HOTEL for DOGS

ALSO BY LOIS DUNCAN

HOTEL FOR DOGS

J pap

BY LOIS DUNCAN

Scholastic Inc.

NEW YORK TORONTO LONDON AUCKLAND SYDNEY

MEXICO CITY NEW DELHI HONG KONG BUENOS AIRES

1/5/12

ISBN-13: 978-0-545-10792-1
ISBN-10: 0-545-10792-X

12 11 10 9 8 7 6 5 4 3 2 1   8 9 10 11 12 13/0

Printed in the U.S.A.
This edition first printing, December 2008

Book design by Tim Hall

In memory of those four-legged members of our family who are now romping happily in Dog Heaven — Ginger, Rascal, Mischief, Kelly, Killer, Scooter, Trixie, Pyrite, and Silver.

CHAPTER ONE

The house was white and square and too small and too perfect.

Bruce studied it from the car window. "Do you suppose there's really room for all of us?" he asked skeptically.

"It looks smug," Andi said. "It has a stuck-up look, as though it thinks it's too good for ordinary people. Even the grass looks fake. I bet it's made of plastic and comes from Home Depot."

"Andi, that is *enough*!" Mr. Walker pulled the car into the driveway and brought it to a stop, but he did not turn off the motor. "You have been acting this way ever since we left New Mexico. We're here now, and in another minute you're going to meet Aunt Alice. I don't want one more unpleasant remark — not *one*."

"Just remember how lucky we are, dear," Mrs. Walker said. "Nobody wants to rent to a family that may only be living in a town for a short time. If Dad's aunt didn't live here and hadn't invited us to stay with her, we might have had to stay behind. You wouldn't have wanted that, would you?"

"Yes," Andi muttered, but she said it under her breath. She did not want to push her luck too far. Besides, she knew she was being unfair and was a little ashamed of herself. The two-story white house in front of them was a perfectly nice place. Actually, some people might have preferred it to the sprawling old adobe they had left behind.

The truth of it was, it was not the house itself that she resented. It was the fact that Bebe would not be allowed to live in it with them.

Until she had discovered that, she had been almost as excited about the thought of the move as Bruce was. Their father's assignment to a new branch of his company meant a big promotion, and they were proud of him and pleased that he was going to Elmwood, New Jersey, for a training program. New people, new experiences, a car trip all the way across the country — how could they *not* have been delighted about those things!

And then their mother had broken the news. She had done it in what Andi thought was a very sneaky way, remarking casually in the middle of packing, "I talked to the Arquettes about keeping Bebe while we're in Elmwood. They say they'll be glad to have her."

"What do you mean?" Andi asked in bewilderment. "Why would they keep Bebe?"

"We won't be able to take her east with us, I'm afraid," Mrs. Walker had said. "Your father's aunt Alice is terribly allergic to dogs."

"*We can't take Bebe!*" Andi had stared at her mother incredulously. Surely she must be joking! Still, this was hardly the sort of thing you joked about. "Bebe's part of our family!"

"She's only a dachshund," Bruce remarked. He was bent over his suitcase, trying to arrange his camera equipment so that nothing would get broken. "That's hardly even a dog. It's more like a noodle."

"It's dog enough for people who are allergic to animals," Mrs. Walker said. "I'm sorry, Andi. I know how you feel, but there's nothing we can do about it. Bebe will have a fine time at the Arquettes'. Holly and her brothers will take good care of her."

"No way! I won't go without her!" Andi had run to Bebe, who was watching all the excitement with interest, and snatched her up in her arms. "If Bebe stays, I will, too!"

"Don't be ridiculous," her mother had said firmly. "As soon as Dad is through with his training and we know where he'll be working, we'll find a place of our own and send for Bebe. I'll be as glad to see that day come as you will. It wasn't easy giving up my teaching position and not being able to apply for a job somewhere else, because we don't know where we're going to end up living."

"I won't go without you, Bebe!" Andi had cried miserably, but, of course, when the time came, she did. When you're ten years old, you go where your parents take you.

Now Mr. Walker turned off the engine and opened the car door.

"Hop out," he said. "And no more sulking. Put on a pleasant face to meet Aunt Alice."

It was at that moment that the door of the house flew open and Aunt Alice herself came rushing out to greet them. Bruce was the first out of the car, and so he was the one Aunt Alice grabbed first.

"So this is my darling great-nephew!" she

cried, clutching him to her. "I haven't seen you since you were a baby, and here you are, almost grown up!"

Bruce, who was actually rather small for his age and embarrassed about it, said, "Hello, Aunt Alice," and tried to pretend he hadn't heard.

Aunt Alice hugged and kissed Mr. and Mrs. Walker next and then fluttered over to Andi.

"And this is sweet little Andrea, who writes such adorable poetry! Your mother sent me one of your dear poems last Christmas!"

This time it was Mrs. Walker who looked embarrassed, because she knew that Andi did not like outsiders to read her poetry, and she had not told her that she had sent a poem to Aunt Alice.

Andi scowled and let Aunt Alice hug her, but she did not hug back.

The inside of the house was just as perfect as the outside. It was so perfect, in fact, that there didn't seem to be any place to sit down that wouldn't get dirty if you touched it.

Mrs. Walker glanced hastily around at the white carpets and lemon-colored sofa and then at the children, who were mussed and grubby from long hours of travel.

"Wouldn't you two like to go outside and explore?" she asked them.

"This is a lovely neighborhood for children," Aunt Alice said. "My neighbors, the Gordons, have a boy just about Bruce's age."

"Do they live in the brown house?" Bruce asked with interest. He had noticed the house as they drove past it and had liked the way it was set off by itself and overgrown with trees and bushes. The grass at that house had not looked fake at all.

"Goodness, no!" Aunt Alice exclaimed. "That old place down by the end of the street? That eyesore has been up for sale for six months now and nobody even stops to look at it. No, the Gordons live right next door in that lovely big house with the garden. Jerry's very popular. There's always a group of boys playing over there."

The September sun was waiting for them when they went outside into the front yard. It fell warm across their heads and shoulders, just as it had back in Albuquerque the day they left. The sky curved rich and blue overhead, and there was a faint, far-off smell of autumn in the air.

"Elmwood isn't really such a bad place," Bruce said. "That house down the street is cool with those vines and bushes all over it, like a hideout in the middle of a forest. I wish we were going to be living there."

"Well, we aren't," Andi said. She was not ready to see the good side of anything. "We're going to be living with allergic Aunt Alice and her white rugs, and I'm going to be 'sweet little Andrea,' and you're going to be 'darling Bruce,' and I don't think I can stand it."

"Don't worry," Bruce said, "you won't be 'sweet Andrea' for long. Not after she gets to know what you're really like. Besides, we'll be at school most of the time, and Dad will be off at work. It will be Mom who has to sit in the house all day and soak it up."

Bruce's camera case hung by a strap from his shoulder. Now he opened it and took out his camera.

"Stand over there by the steps, and I'll get your picture. You can send it to Holly Arquette to show to Bebe."

"All right," Andi said more agreeably. It wasn't often that Bruce offered to photograph his sister. Usually he concentrated on more interesting subject matter.

She had been standing by the porch steps for about thirty seconds when she heard Bruce say, "Hey!"

"Hey, what?" Andi asked him.

"Hey, look who's come visiting! He wants his picture taken. Look at him pose!"

Andi turned to find her brother aiming his camera, not at her, but at a big red dog who stood surveying them from the line between Aunt Alice's house and the one she had told them belonged to the Gordons.

"Where did he come from?" Andi asked, too surprised to feel insulted because she would no longer be the subject of the picture.

"I don't know, but he shouldn't be out wandering. He's a beauty, isn't he?" Shifting his camera to his left hand, Bruce held his right one out to the dog. "Here, boy, come over and see me. Do you live around here?"

Waving his full red tail like a welcoming banner, the dog came eagerly forward to meet his new friend. Dropping to his knees, Bruce took the soft face in his hands and smiled into its brown eyes.

"I didn't think you liked dogs all that much," Andi said. "You never spend time playing with Bebe."

"Bebe's spoiled," Bruce said. "She doesn't want to play, she just wants to be petted. This big fellow is a man's dog. I bet he'd be fun to take —"

"What do you think you're doing with my dog?" The coldness of the voice cut like a knife through the soft afternoon.

Bruce glanced up in surprise at the tall, blond-haired boy who was suddenly standing in front of him.

"Hi," he said in his friendly way. "You must be Jerry Gordon. Aunt Alice said you lived next door. I'm Bruce Walker, and that's my sister, Andi. We're going to be your neighbors for a while."

"I didn't ask who you were," the boy said curtly. "I asked you what you think you're doing with Red Rover. That's an expensive dog with a mile-long pedigree. My dad gave him to me for my birthday, and nobody messes around with him without my permission."

"Bruce isn't hurting him. All he did was take his picture." Andi left her place by the steps and came across the lawn to join the two boys. "I don't think this is your dog anyway. If he was, he wouldn't be acting like that."

At the sound of the boy's voice the dog had pressed himself tightly against Bruce's leg.

"He's mine, all right," Jerry Gordon said. He snapped his fingers. "Come on, Red. Get over there in your own yard."

Instead of obeying, the dog dropped his head and whined nervously. He seemed to huddle even harder against Bruce, as though begging for protection.

"What's the matter with him?" Bruce asked. "I've never seen my sister's dog act like that. She comes leaping when Andi calls her."

"He's stubborn," the tall boy said. "I haven't got him trained yet. Red Rover, you get over there, do you hear me?"

Raising his hand, he brought it down in a hard stroke between the dog's shoulder blades. Red Rover gave a yelp of pain. Dashing past his master, he ran across the yard and disappeared around the corner of the house.

"Is that what you call training?" Bruce gave a snort of disgust. "No wonder the poor thing's scared of you. He'll end up hating you if you keep on treating him that way."

"You don't deserve to have a dog!" Andi's voice was choked with fury. "If I was Red Rover, I'd bite your arm off!"

"He's got to learn to obey," Jerry Gordon said. "You've got to show a dog who's boss. If he acts like he ought to, then I'm nice to him." He paused and then added in a more pleasant voice, "That goes for people, too. You behave yourself, and maybe I'll let you come over sometime." He nodded at Bruce. "You, I mean. Your dorky sister is something else."

"What makes you think I'd come if you invited me?" Bruce asked. "Maybe I'd rather look for other friends."

"Sure you'd come," Jerry said confidently. "All the guys in the neighborhood want to hang out at my place. I've got more cool stuff than the rest of you put together. They're not going to risk getting in bad with me by being friends with a shrimp like you."

"My brother's not a shrimp!" Andi said angrily. "He's a straight-A student and an awesome photographer! Everybody likes Bruce! Back in Albuquerque he was voted president of his class!"

"Maybe you western weirdo types like shrimp," Jerry said. "Here in the East we eat them for dinner. And we don't much like fat little girls, especially when they talk funny."

"I am not fat!" cried Andi, who really wasn't — only a little plump and not nearly as much as she had been when she was younger. "And I don't talk funny! You're the one with a stupid accent!"

"Ah don't tawk funnnnnnnny!" Jerry gave an imitation of a western drawl like the ones on TV shows. Then suddenly his eyes lifted, and the sneering expression left his face. In its place there appeared the sweetest smile imaginable.

"Hi, Mrs. Scudder!" he called. "How are you today?"

Bruce and Andi turned simultaneously to see Aunt Alice standing on the front porch with their parents close behind her. She was evidently bringing the Walkers out to show them her garden.

"Just fine, Jerry, dear," she called back, her face breaking into a broad smile at the sight of the three children together. "I'm so happy you've met each other! I was telling Bruce and Andi that we have the sweetest boy next door. I was coming out to introduce you, but I see that you're friends already!"

CHAPTER TWO

For Andi, the hardest part about starting her new school was the fact that Bruce was not starting it with her. For as long as she could remember, Andi had depended on her brother to make friends for both of them.

Now Bruce was a whole mile away at Elmwood Middle School. It was a terrible, lonely feeling not to have him to lean on. Andi, who was never at ease with strangers, found herself acting stiffer than ever.

On her first day at the new school a blond, bright-faced girl named Debbie Austin had come up to her on the playground and asked if she wanted to play a game called "Double Trouble." Andi, who had never heard of the game and was embarrassed to admit it, had responded, "No, thank you."

"Oh, come on," Debbie coaxed her. "It isn't much harder than 'Singles.' You'll catch on fast."

"I'm really not interested," Andi told her.

Debbie had walked off, looking hurt, and Andi had been furious with herself, especially when she saw the little group of girls playing double jump rope. It was a game that she had often played back in Albuquerque, and she'd actually been pretty good at it, but she'd never heard it referred to as "Double Trouble." Now that she realized what it was, she was dying to rush over and say, "Oh, I do want to play after all!"

When she thought about doing that, though, something knotted up inside her and she simply couldn't. Instead, when Debbie or any of the other girls glanced in her direction, she stared straight through them as though she didn't see them.

Nobody ever asked her to play jump rope again.

So even though it was her own fault and she knew it, Andi found herself at the end of her first week at Elmwood Elementary School without a single friend.

At home, she pretended.

"We had such fun on the playground today," she told the family at dinner, or, "You should have heard the jokes the girls were telling me at lunch!"

Then she felt guilty when Aunt Alice turned to her mother and said, "Linda, you and John are fortunate to have such a popular daughter! Imagine making so many new friends so quickly!"

But the thing Andi missed the most in the entire world was Bebe. Bebe had been her dog for almost three years now. She had gotten her for Christmas the year she was eight, when Bebe was just a puppy, so tiny that it had hardly seemed possible that she was real.

She had been under the tree in a box all wrapped with Christmas paper, with little holes in the sides so that air could get through. Andi had unwrapped the paper and felt the box move. Then the lid had popped off, and there had been Bebe, pointed little face all bright and sparkling, nose wiggling, eyes shining, tail long and thin like a piece of black wire thumping against the bottom of the box.

"We got Bruce a digital camera, but we thought you would like this better," Mr. Walker had said, laughing at the startled look on his daughter's face.

Then, as though she had heard and understood the words, Bebe had jumped out of the box right into Andi's arms, and from then on there had been nobody else for either of them. Many people might like Bruce best, but not Bebe. Bebe thought there was nobody in the world as wonderful as Andi.

I wish she was here now, Andi thought as she left the classroom and walked down the long hallway to the outside door. All around her, boys and girls rushed by with arms filled with books, laughing and chattering, calling to one another, "Wait up! Wait for me!" It seemed to Andi that she was the only one in the whole school who had no friends to walk with when the final bell rang.

I'll pretend Bebe is out there, she told herself. *I'll pretend she's waiting right outside the door.*

That thought made her feel oddly better, and when she had walked out the door and there was no little dog standing there, she told herself, *She's waiting a little farther on, down by the street.*

When she reached the street, she thought, *No — she didn't come this far. She's still at home in the corner of the yard, keeping her eyes on the sidewalk, hoping I'll be coming.*

Andi thought about Bebe all the way home. She thought about her so hard that she found herself getting more and more homesick. By the time she reached her own block, her eyes were swimming in tears and she could hardly keep from sobbing out loud.

She hurried along the sidewalk, staring straight ahead of her — past the rows of maple trees, already beginning to redden with the chill of autumn nights, past the overgrown brown house with its "FOR SALE" sign out front, past a vacant lot and a yellow house with curtains over its windows — and turned up the neat white path that led to Aunt Alice's front door.

Then she stopped. She could not believe her eyes. There on the porch steps, sitting in a forlorn little heap as though he were waiting for someone, was a dog.

"Bebe?" Andi spoke softly, almost afraid that the sound of her voice would make the dog disappear. Wiping the tears from her eyes with the back of her hand, she crept up the walk until she was only a few feet away.

Now that she was close, she could see that the dog was not Bebe, was not even a bit like Bebe, really, except for the color, which was brown, and the small size. This was a shaggy dog with long, dirty, uncombed hair hanging in all directions.

"Hi there, little dog," Andi said softly. "Are you waiting for me?"

The bundle of hair turned so that what seemed to be the front of the head was facing Andi, and from somewhere at the back of the bundle something began to twitch in what Andi thought must be a wag.

Reaching out, she pushed aside the hair that covered the dog's face, and there, gazing soulfully up at her, were two bright button eyes.

"What are you doing, waiting here?" Andi asked. "Are you hungry? Come on, you poor little thing. Andi will get you something to eat."

Gathering the dog up in her arms, she carried him through the house to the kitchen.

Her mother was there peeling carrots. Mrs. Walker had fallen into the habit of doing the early part of the dinner preparations when she could have the kitchen to herself while Aunt Alice was upstairs taking her afternoon nap.

"Andi, no!" she exclaimed when she saw Andi standing in the doorway. "Take that dog right back outside!"

"But, Mom, he's hungry," Andi told her. "We can't let a sweet thing like this starve to death right on our front steps. Can't I give him a bowl of milk?"

"No, you can't," Mrs. Walker said firmly. "If you do that you'll be encouraging him to stay. When you feed a stray animal you're inviting it to make itself at home."

"Just a little milk, Mom?" Andi begged. "Please? Just think if this was Bebe, all hungry and nobody feeding her —" Her eyes began to get teary again at the thought.

"Well, he's not Bebe," Mrs. Walker said. "He probably has a perfectly good home around here and just wandered away from it. Now, take him back outside and give him a little shove to get him moving. Maybe he'll take himself home in time for dinner."

"He doesn't have a home," Andi said with certainty. "He doesn't have a collar or tag or anything, and he's so dirty and shabby and neglected —"

"Outside, Andi," Mrs. Walker said. "Now! Before Aunt Alice comes down from her nap and gets a sneezing spell. This is her home, honey, and we are her houseguests. We have to live by Aunt Alice's rules and fit into her way of doing things."

"Oh, all right," Andi said mournfully, and carried the dog outside.

"Poor baby," she murmured, rocking him back and forth in her arms. "Poor little unwanted thing!"

Glancing up the street to the left, she said, "There's no sense sending you off in that direction. The people who own the yellow house are off on vacation or something, and there's the vacant lot and the empty brown house. The other direction's worse." She gave a shudder as she turned to the right. "That horrid Gordon boy lives there. He'd probably pull your legs off."

Looking across the street, she noticed a pleasant gray house with a swing set in the side yard and bicycles parked out front.

"Maybe you'll find a home there," she said, trying to sound hopeful. "At least, it looks like your best bet."

Carrying the dog gently, she crossed the street and set him down in front of the gray house and gave him a little push in the direction of the porch. Then, quickly so that he would not follow her, she ran back across the street.

A new thought struck her just as she ran up the steps. *What if Bebe ran away! What if she ran away from the Arquettes and set off to find me! What if she's out wandering now, just like that poor dog, with nobody to feed or care for her!*

It was such a dreadful thought that she felt sick to her stomach. Hurrying into the house, she rushed up the stairs to the room that was hers — it had been Aunt Alice's sewing room, but it contained a couch that folded down into a bed — and flew inside and slammed the door.

On the table by the bed were a pencil and note pad. Snatching them up, Andi threw herself across the couch and began to compose a poem. "Bebe" was the title, and the words came pouring out, hurling themselves upon the paper:

> *Weeping through the morning mists,*
> *I wandered all alone,*
> *Searching for the only thing*
> *That I could call my own.*

Whenever she was upset, Andi wrote poetry, and by now she had a large collection of poems. She wrote when she was happy, too, and sometimes when she was bored, but those poems never seemed to turn out as well as the ones she wrote when she was miserable.

When her poems were completed, she copied them neatly onto clean paper and sent them off to *Good Housekeeping* and *The New Yorker*, which had been magazines on her parents' coffee table at home. She had started doing that the year she turned nine. She had heard somewhere once that Shakespeare had written his first play by the time he was eleven, and she had made up her mind that if she reached the age of eleven without having had a poem published, she would give up writing and turn to something else.

Sometimes poems were hard to write, and sometimes they were easy, but because she was already so worked up and filled with feelings, Andi found that this poem was the easiest she had ever written. Words came spilling out onto the page without her even having to think about them.

She was just finishing the last line when there was a rap on the door.

"Andi?" It was Bruce's voice. "Mom wants you to come down and set the table."

"Is it that time already?" Andi glanced up in astonishment to see dusk hanging heavy outside the window. "I didn't even know you were home."

Sliding the paper into her notebook, she got up and stretched. She felt good, as though all the unhappiness that had been inside her had drained off onto that sheet of paper. Tossing the notebook back onto the table, she left the room and went downstairs.

It began to rain as she set the table for dinner. It started as just a sprinkle, the lightest, slightest sound, like a gentle tap-tap-tap on the roof. By the time she had the napkins and silverware on, however, the tapping had increased to a roar.

"I'd better check the upstairs windows," Bruce said and went up to the second floor. "Dad's coming," he called down a moment later. "I can see his car."

"I hope he took an umbrella with him," Mrs. Walker called from the kitchen, where she was helping Aunt Alice with the mashed potatoes.

The drum of the rain drowned out the sound of the car in the driveway, but they all heard Mr. Walker's feet as they thudded on the porch steps. Andi left the table and ran to open the door for him.

He came in dripping and shaking himself the way he would have in the brick hallway back home. Then he realized what he was doing and said, "Oh, my gosh, the rugs!"

"Quick — get newspapers! A bath mat! Bruce, run for some towels!" Aunt Alice came fluttering out of the kitchen to dab helplessly with the corner of a dish towel at the dampness on the snowy carpet.

Behind her father, Andi saw the water falling in a solid sheet as heavy and loud as a waterfall. Mr. Walker was shoving his wet hair back from his face. Bruce was rushing down the stairs, his arms filled with bath towels. Mrs. Walker was hurrying in from the kitchen with a roll of paper towels, her face creased with worry.

"Oh, dear," she was saying. "I hope the carpet doesn't stain!"

They were all so occupied that there was one thing they did not see. Andi saw it, and she opened her mouth to speak. Then, slowly, she closed it again. *I'm not going to say a word,* she thought, as the little brown dog with the long wet hair came scampering in the door between her father's feet and scurried down the hall and up the stairs.

CHAPTER THREE

At dinner that night Andi could not keep her attention on what was going on at the table. Conversation drifted around her, hardly touching her ears.

The food on her plate sat there getting colder and colder until her mother said, "Earth to Andi! Are you off somewhere in space, honey? Is something the matter? Don't you feel well?"

"Oh, no—no—I feel fine." Hurriedly, Andi picked up her fork and began to eat. "I was just thinking."

Actually she had not been thinking at all—she had been listening. The smell of roast beef on the serving platter rolled out in warm, mouthwatering waves through the lower part of the house. *How long would it be,* she wondered, *before the odor floated up the stairs to where a hungry dog was hiding? When it did, how long could he resist it?*

She could almost hear the click of toenails on the stairs as a bundle of wet hair came scurrying down to beg for some supper.

Stay there, she willed silently. *Stay there and wait a little longer. Andi will bring some dinner up to you soon.*

As though she were reading her daughter's thoughts, Mrs. Walker said, "Andi is upset because she found a little stray dog this afternoon and I wouldn't let her bring it into the house. She is so used to having her own dog around to play with that it is a little hard for her to understand that it's just not possible here."

"Oh, mercy, no!" Aunt Alice raised her napkin to her face as though waving away the very thought of such a disaster. "I cannot get anywhere near animal hair. Even bird hair — I mean, feathers — I can't have them in the house either. All my pillows are foam rubber."

"How about fish?" Bruce asked with interest. "Can you get near them?"

"I don't know," Aunt Alice admitted. "I've never been brave enough to try." She turned to Andi. "If you miss your pet so much, dear, why don't you go next door to play? Jerry has a beautiful Irish setter. His parents just gave it to him recently."

"I don't think I'd like to play there," Andi said.

"Not like it at Jerry's!" Aunt Alice gave a gasp of astonishment. "Why, you should see how his parents have fixed up the whole basement floor for Jerry and his friends! It's just beautiful — all pine paneled, with Jerry's bedroom down there and a game room with a pool table and big-screen TV and, goodness, I don't know what all. I can't understand why you children aren't over there playing every day!"

"Jerry and I didn't hit it off," Bruce said shortly.

The statement was so out of character coming from Bruce that the adults at the table turned to stare at him.

"That's not like you," Mr. Walker said. "You've never had any problem making friends with other boys."

"I don't want Jerry Gordon for a friend," Bruce said. "You should see the way he treats his poor dog."

"Oh, Bruce, I'm sure you're mistaken!" Aunt Alice exclaimed. "The Gordons are lovely people! I can't imagine a boy like Jerry mistreating a pet."

"You wouldn't think it to see him around grown-ups," Bruce acknowledged. "They always give him his way, so he's real polite and nice. With his dog he's different. Red Rover's scared to death of him, isn't he, Andi?" He turned to his sister for support.

"What?" Andi had not heard the question. Stuffing the last forkful of food into her mouth, she almost sighed aloud with relief. "Please, may I be excused?"

"Not until the rest of us are finished," her mother said. "Then you can help clear the table and load the dishwasher."

Andi started to object, and then an idea occurred to her.

"I'll do the kitchen myself," she said. "The rest of you can relax. I'll take care of everything."

"Why, Andi!" Her mother looked stunned.

"Isn't that lovely!" Aunt Alice cried in delight. "What a helpful little girl you are!"

Bruce, for his part, was staring at his sister as if she had gone crazy.

Andi had just finished scrubbing the pans when her brother came into the kitchen. Closing the door behind him, he confronted her.

"Okay. Let's have it. What's the gimmick?"

"What do you mean, 'gimmick'?" Andi asked uneasily. "I just thought I'd save Mom and Aunt Alice some work and —"

"Come off it," Bruce said firmly. "Aunt Alice may think you're a 'helpful little girl,' but I know better. What's that you're hiding under your sweatshirt? Come on, now —"

"Nothing," Andi insisted, trying to duck away from him, but he was too fast for her. He caught hold of the shirt and pulled it up.

"A dish of roast beef?"

"I — I thought —" Andi stumbled for an explanation. "I thought I might want a bedtime snack."

"That's a lie and you know it!" Bruce could always tell when she was lying. "What's the beef for? You'd better tell me."

"Oh, all right," Andi said reluctantly. "You'll have to promise, though, that you won't tell."

"Won't tell who?"

"Anybody. Mom, Dad — especially Aunt Alice. This is a very deep secret. It's a matter of life and death."

"Okay, I promise." Bruce's curiosity could be contained no longer. "What is it?"

"I have a dog upstairs," Andi whispered.

"That stray Mom said you found? You brought it in here, after all?" There was grudging respect in Bruce's voice. "When did you manage to do that? Where do you have him?"

"I don't know exactly," Andi said. "He's someplace upstairs. He ran up right before dinner. I haven't had a chance to go up there. You should see him, Bruce — he's so pitiful, all wet and hungry with nobody to love him."

"Well, come on, then," Bruce said. "Let's take the food up to him now while they're all in the den watching TV."

Andi smiled at her brother gratefully. She was never certain how Bruce was going to react to things. Sometimes he was her closest friend, cooperating with anything she suggested, and other times he acted stuffy and self-righteous, almost like a grown-up. This time, thank heaven, he was going to be all right.

"Let's go," she said, pulling her shirt down over the plate again.

The noise from the dishwasher and the television set in the den drowned out the sound of their footsteps as they mounted the stairs. In the second-floor hallway Andi stopped and set down the dish of beef.

"Here, doggie!" she called softly. "Come here, dear! Andi has something nice for you!"

Only silence greeted her voice.

"That's weird," Bruce said. "If he's as hungry as you say, you'd think he'd come running. Dogs have good noses. They can tell when you have food."

"Maybe he's asleep," Andi said. "He's done a lot of running around today, poor thing, and he's probably exhausted. You start at this end, and I'll start on the other, and we'll find him."

Systematically, they began a search of the second floor. Bruce's area consisted of Aunt Alice's big bedroom and a storage closet and bathroom. Andi's included the guest room, which was now being used by their parents, and the sewing room. They met at last in the center of the hallway with blank faces.

"No sign of any dog that I can see," Bruce said. "I checked under beds and behind curtains and everywhere."

"He doesn't seem to be at this end of the hall." Andi frowned. "Let's switch. I'll look through all the rooms you looked through, and you look through mine. One of us must have missed him."

"I'm sure I didn't," Bruce said, but he began a search of their parents' bedroom while Andi started on Aunt Alice's.

She went through it carefully, looking inside and behind things, slithering on her stomach to look under the bed, parting the curtains of the fluffy pink dressing table that looked like something out of an old-fashioned movie.

As she moved about, she kept calling in a soft voice, "Here, doggie! Come out, little doggie!"

By the time she had gone through the bathroom, looking in the tub, in the dirty clothes hamper, and behind the toilet, she was beginning to wonder if the dog was some kind of magician and had vanished into thin air.

Bruce seemed to be feeling the same way.

"Are you sure he's here?" he asked. "Maybe he ran down again when you weren't looking."

"I don't see how he could have," Andi told him. "From where I was sitting at the table, I could see down the hall to the foot of the stairs. Besides, if he'd come down, it would have been straight into the dining room. That's where the food was."

"Well, he doesn't seem to be around now," Bruce said. "Maybe you daydreamed him. Maybe you wanted to see a dog so much that you made yourself think you saw one."

"That's stupid," Andi said. This was the kind of grown-up comment Bruce sometimes made that caused her to want to slap him. "I didn't daydream anything. That dog is up here somewhere."

"I don't see how —" Bruce began, when their mother's voice rang from downstairs.

"Children? Have you taken your showers yet?"

"No," they called back in unison.

"Then go ahead and take them. It's almost bedtime."

"Okay!" Bruce dropped his voice again. "I've done all the hunting I'm going to do. I don't believe there is any dog. Dibs on the first shower."

"No, you don't. You took the first one last night and used up all the hot water." Andi picked up the plate of food from the floor and hurried to the sewing room. Once inside, she flicked on the light and got out her nightshirt. Then she glanced around for a place to hide the dish. It would not do to have it sitting out when her mother came up to say good night.

The door to the sewing closet on the far side of the room gaped open a crack. This closet was the place where Aunt Alice kept her patterns and materials. Crossing the room, Andi pulled the door wide open and set the dish down on top of a pile of patterns. She was just turning away when her eye was caught by a movement in the corner.

"So, there you are!" Andi dropped to her knees on the closet floor. "No wonder we couldn't find you! You've got yourself hidden under a pile of material!"

Reaching over, she began to pull the cloth aside. "Why, you've made it into a kind of nest. What do you think you are, you silly thing, a bird? Don't you know that Aunt Alice is allergic to feathers just like dog hair, and she —"

Andi stopped short. Then she caught her breath in a startled gasp. There in the soft bed she had made for herself was not only the shaggy brown dog, but three tiny brown-and-white puppies.

CHAPTER FOUR

"I don't care," Andi said. "You can't break a promise, Bruce, no matter what."

"But don't you see, I didn't know what I was promising! If I'd known, I wouldn't have promised."

Bruce regarded his sister with exasperation. Andi was the most interesting person he knew, even if she was part of his family. There were things wrong with her, to be sure — she was always shutting herself off someplace with her scribbling, and she had a bad temper, and sometimes she told lies. But she was never boring. Most of the boys he knew complained about their sisters being drags. With Andi it was just the opposite; she never dragged. Sometimes, like now, Bruce almost wished that she did.

"Look, sis," he said as patiently as he could, "you know as well as I do that we can't keep dogs here.

Mom and Dad explained it to us before we left home, and you heard Aunt Alice at dinner tonight. All you have to do is mention the word 'dog' and her nose starts dripping."

"I don't know why you're acting this way," Andi said. "You didn't start lecturing out in the kitchen. You said that you'd help me find the dog and feed her."

"Well, sure, I wanted to feed her," Bruce said reasonably. "I wouldn't want any animal to starve. I could see letting her in out of a rainstorm, too. *Keeping* her here is something else. We can't do that. Besides, it's not just one dog now — it's four."

"What do you want to do, throw them out on the street?" Andi asked, trying to sound reasonable also. "With those little puppies just an hour old? And the nights turning cold — and maybe more rain — and nothing to eat —"

"If we told Dad and Mom —" Bruce began.

"What could they do? You can't find homes for puppies this little; they have to stay with their mother. You know what the grown-ups would do. They'd send them to the pound."

"Oh, no!" Bruce said. This was something he had not thought about. He had gone with his parents to the pound in Albuquerque the day they got Bebe for Andi's Christmas present. He still could remember the cages of sad-faced animals, all waiting hopefully for somebody to adopt them.

"I'll tell you what," he said slowly. "We won't do anything tonight. The dogs are all settled, and nobody has to know about them. In the morning, of course, there'll be a problem. After we leave for school, Mom or Aunt Alice might come in here —"

"I won't go to school," Andi said. "I'll have a stomachache."

"I guess you could do that," Bruce agreed. "Mom always believes your stomachaches, and that way you could keep the door closed and say you wanted to sleep. That would give me a day to come up with some kind of plan. I hope I can do it in a day."

"Oh, I'm sure you can," Andi said confidently. She smiled, all the worry gone from her face.

Bruce, himself, was not nearly so certain. He stayed awake a long time that night thinking about the problem, and he concentrated on it so hard at school the next day that he missed three questions on his math quiz. Math had always been easy for

Bruce, so he was shocked when the teacher called out the grades.

From his seat in the next row, Jerry Gordon turned and grinned. It was such a pleased grin that Bruce was angrier with himself than ever.

It had been an unpleasant surprise on the first day of school to find Jerry in the class with him. It had been a shock for Jerry as well.

"What are you doing here?" he had asked that first morning, when the two boys had found themselves side by side in the same homeroom. "You're not big enough for middle school."

"I was twelve in February," Bruce told him coldly.

"Nobody would guess it. You look like you ought to be in kindergarten."

"Boys!" Miss Lowry had spoken from the front of the room.

At the sound of her voice, Jerry's expression changed completely. Glancing up quickly, he gave the teacher a warm, bright smile.

"I'm sorry, Miss Lowry. I was just trying to help our new student feel at home."

"That was nice of you, Jerry." Miss Lowry's stern face softened. "You're very thoughtful, and I know Bruce appreciates it. Let's save our chatting for the playground and lunchroom, though. Okay?"

"Sure, Miss Lowry." Jerry dropped his eyes as though embarrassed. Under his lowered lids he shot Bruce a side glance.

"Save your chatting for the playground, shrimp, if you can find anybody to chat with," he whispered, as Miss Lowry turned her attention to a student on the other side of the room. "You're going to have a hard time finding any buds in this class, I can promise you that."

As days went by, the statement had turned out to be more true than Bruce had expected. Jerry Gordon was the leader of the neighborhood gang, which seemed to consist of most of the boys in the seventh grade. On the playground, it was Jerry who chose what games they played and told people which sides they were on, and it was Jerry who organized the after-school activities and conducted special meetings in the basement of his home.

"What's with that guy?" Bruce asked Tim Kelly, who sat in front of him in history class. "People jump when he gives orders like he was king of Elmwood."

"Nobody wants to make him mad, that's for sure. If he doesn't like you, he can make life pretty tough." Tim had a shock of red hair and the kind of open, freckled face that made Bruce wish he knew him better.

"Jerry *is* sort of like a king around here," he continued. "He's an only kid, and his parents don't say no to anything. He's got the whole basement floor of the house for his own. He can have all the guys he wants over there, and nobody ever bothers him." He laughed. "It's different at my house. I've got three little sisters. Nothing's private over there."

"I've got a sister, too," Bruce said. "She bugs me sometimes, but I'd sure rather have her around than Jerry Gordon."

"Oh, he's not so bad if you don't cross him," Tim said. "He can be real charming and nice to people he likes." He paused. "Of course, when things don't go his way, that's different. Like with the kid who used to live in that house down the street from you, the one that's for sale now."

"What about him?" Bruce asked curiously. "What happened?"

"I hear that Jerry had a run-in with the kid. I

don't know what it was about; it was before our family moved here. Anyway, from the way I heard it, Jerry made life so miserable for that kid that he got where he wouldn't go to school. None of the other kids would have anything to do with him for fear of making Jerry mad. Finally, the family moved to a different school district. Before they left, though, the kid's dad went over and had a show-down with Mr. Gordon and told him how rotten Jerry was."

"Wow!" It made Bruce feel good just to imagine that confrontation. "What did Mr. Gordon do?"

"Nothing." Tim shrugged. "He didn't believe it. Grown-ups never see that side of Jerry. The Gordons think he's perfect. Anyway, Jerry got so steamed up when he learned what the kid's dad had said about him that he went over to the house and threw rocks through all the back windows."

Bruce was appalled. "Why do you hang out with him?" he asked incredulously. "You trail him around on the playground, just like the rest of them do."

"Well, he's never done anything to me person-ally." Tim looked a little embarrassed. "We just moved to Elmwood last spring. All the guys I met here were in Jerry's gang. When you're new in a place, you don't have a lot of choices. You hang out with whoever's there. It's no fun being a loner."

"I'd rather be a loner than hang out with some-body like Jerry," Bruce said firmly.

There was a moment that afternoon, though, when he did not feel quite so definite. The last bell had rung, and as he left the building, Bruce saw a group of boys headed toward the park across the street. Tim was with them, and he was carrying a football.

As he reached the curb, Tim glanced back and saw Bruce watching them. He smiled and waved and gestured for Bruce to join them. For a moment Bruce was tempted. He had not played football yet this season. He was small for his age, but he was fast, and when he got the ball, he could usually leave the larger players behind. It would be fun —

Then he glanced beyond Tim and saw the boy who headed the group. Quickly, he shook his head. No matter how much he wanted to play, he would not go crawling over to beg permission from Jerry Gordon. Giving Tim a rueful smile, he headed off toward home.

The middle school was closer to Aunt Alice's house than the grade school that Andi attended, so in reality Bruce did not have very far to walk. It seemed a long way, however, when walking alone. Bruce was used to having friends, and the lack of them now was even harder for him than for Andi. She could shut herself off and write poetry and lose track of time, but Bruce had no such talent. For him the after-school hours dragged, endless with their emptiness.

Bruce walked slowly; there was nothing to hurry home for. When he came to the brown house with the "FOR SALE" sign, he regarded it with interest.

I bet that kid was glad to move away from here, he thought sympathetically. *I'll be glad myself when Dad finds out where he's going to be working.*

He remembered Tim's statement about the back windows. Could Jerry really have been angry enough to break every one of them? It was hard to imagine, but there was no reason for Tim to have lied about it. Anyway, Tim did not appear to be the sort of boy who made up stories about people.

Bruce hesitated and then, as his curiosity got the better of him, left the sidewalk and walked around to the far side of the house.

The moment he left the front yard, the bushes seemed to close in on him. They rose on all sides, untrimmed and untended, surrounding him like a jungle. The whole backyard was overgrown with knee-high grass and brambles and vines gone wild from neglect.

All the first-floor windows in the back of the house gaped empty, and piles of broken glass lay under them, glinting in the afternoon sunlight.

"What a mess!" Bruce regarded the destruction with disgust. "Somebody ought to report this to the police."

For one lovely moment he let himself toy with the idea of being the one to do it. It was a nice thought, and he enjoyed it before setting it aside for cold reality. He had no proof that Jerry was the one who had broken the windows. Tim himself had only heard about it from other people. Jerry would deny it, of course, and look innocent, and give that wide, sweet smile that always melted grown-ups, and the police would not believe it, and certainly the Gordons wouldn't.

Discarding the idea regretfully, Bruce waded through the tall grass to inspect the damage more closely. Jerry had done a thorough job, all right.

All that remained of the windows were some jagged slivers of glass that were still stuck in the frames.

Working with care so as not to cut himself on the sharp edges, Bruce began to remove those. They could be dangerous, he told himself. Some little kid might come around here and decide to crawl in to explore.

The windows were set low and would be easy to straddle. Looking in, Bruce could see an empty room with a door standing open to a hallway. Beyond that was another room with the door closed.

Dust lay thick over everything. How long had Aunt Alice said the house had stood empty? Six months, without anyone even coming to look at it?

It was too bad for a place to stay vacant like this, Bruce thought. There must be people in the world without a home who would be glad to look after the place just for a chance to sleep there.

It was then that the idea hit him. It came suddenly, like a great floodlight going on in his brain. It was the answer to everything.

For a moment he stood contemplating. Would it work? There would be plenty of problems. Still, even with problems, it seemed better than anything else they could come up with.

Tossing the last of the glass fragments into the bushes, he turned and began to run through the row of maples, across the vacant lot, toward Aunt Alice's neat white house down the street.

CHAPTER FIVE

It was on a Friday afternoon that the dogs moved in.

"And that's what I'm naming her," Andi said. "I'm going to name her Friday, because that's the day she's getting her very own home. Oh, Bruce, this was the most wonderful idea! Friday and her puppies will think they're staying in a hotel!"

"Well, they'd better not get too used to it," Bruce said. "As soon as the pups are old enough, we're going to find homes for all of them and for Friday, too."

He spoke decisively to cover the fact that he was beginning to feel a little nervous. The idea had seemed so reasonable when it first occurred to him: a vacant house with no one to tend it, four little dogs that needed a place to stay, so why not put them together for a few weeks?

The thing that was not reasonable was the way Andi was acting. In the day she had spent at home having her stomachache, she had formed a deep attachment to the group in the sewing closet. And now she was giving them names as if she expected to be their mistress for the rest of her life.

"This is just a short-term emergency thing," Bruce kept saying, as he followed her about from one empty room to another. "This is somebody else's property, even if they're not living here. We really shouldn't be using it at all."

"I know, I know." Andi's eyes were shining with excitement. "I think Friday would like the pink bedroom at the front of the hotel, don't you? It's such a ladylike room, and that big window lets in so much light. We can fix her a bed in the corner, and when the puppies start walking, they can go exploring down the hall to the living room."

"By the time they can do that, they'll be ready to leave," Bruce said. "We should start right now trying to line up homes for them. Does your school have a bulletin board? You could pin up a sort of announcement —"

But Andi was gone again, hurrying through to the kitchen to see if the faucets were working. It would be so much easier to fill Friday's drinking bowl from there than to have to keep carrying water over from Aunt Alice's.

Andi was up at dawn the next morning and out of the house before anyone else was awake. Mrs. Walker discovered her room empty when she went to call her to breakfast.

"I can't understand it," she said in bewilderment as she joined the rest of the family at the breakfast table. "Andi never gets up early if she can help it. Where in the world could she have gone?"

"Perhaps she's over at somebody's house," Mr. Walker suggested. "From the way she talks, she has dozens of girlfriends."

"This early in the morning?" Mrs. Walker shook her head. "Nobody goes visiting before breakfast." She turned to Bruce. "Did your sister say anything to you about having plans for this morning?"

"I — I don't think so. I mean, I don't exactly remember." Bruce felt his face growing hot. He had never been able to tell a lie successfully, even a little one.

"I do hope she doesn't stay out too long," Aunt Alice said. "Surely she knows that Saturday is cleaning day. There's so much dust in the air these days

that we have to keep ahead of it, don't we?"
She gave a little sniff and reached for her handker-
chief. "My poor nose! My allergies have been so
bad these past few days. I can't imagine what's caus-
ing it."

By the time breakfast was over and Andi still
had not returned, Mrs. Walker was looking truly
worried.

"Really, Bruce," she said, drawing him aside, "do
you have any idea where Andi might have gone?
It's so unlike her to miss a meal, and besides, she
does know that Aunt Alice feels strongly about
Saturday cleaning."

"We cleaned last Saturday and the Saturday before
that," Bruce said. "Geez, Mom, we haven't had a
chance to get anything dirty!"

"I know," Mrs. Walker said with a sigh, "but it
must seem that way to Aunt Alice. She's lived alone
for so long that just normal tracking in and out
brings in more dirt than she's used to. Besides, dust
does seem to bother her terribly. The poor thing has
been sneezing constantly."

"It's not the dust," Bruce said. "It's the —"
He stopped himself. How could he possibly tell

his mother, "it's the dog hair, and the dogs are gone now"?

"Okay," he said reluctantly, "if Aunt Alice says it's cleaning day, I guess that's it. There's no reason Andi should be able to goof off when the rest of us can't. I'll go hunt her down."

Actually, Bruce was more irritated at Andi than his mother was. He knew exactly where she was and what she was doing, and he thought it was a dirty trick for her to have run off on a Saturday and leave him behind to field questions about her whereabouts.

As he left the house and started toward the hotel, he rehearsed under his breath the things he was going to say to her.

"Those dogs can get along by themselves until we've got the chores done. If you start pulling this sort of stuff, you're going to ruin everything. People are going to wonder what we're doing, and then we'll be in for it. Mom's already asking questions."

He was so intent on the speech he was planning that he was not aware of another presence until a voice called out to him, "Hey, shrimp, do you always go around talking to yourself?"

Turning with a start, he saw Jerry Gordon standing only a few yards away from him. Three other boys were with him. One of them was Tim, who smiled and waved good-naturedly.

"Hi, Bruce! Where are you going in such a hurry?"

"Oh, just — well — my sister's wandered off someplace." Ignoring Jerry, Bruce responded to the more pleasant greeting. "My mother asked me to go round her up."

"Like a cow on a ranch?" Jerry threw out the insult like a challenge.

Bruce fought back the temptation to be drawn into a name-calling contest. Squaring his shoulders, he was about to walk on past when a flash of red caught his eye and he saw Jerry's dog there with him. The dog was on a lead and had a rope tied across his chest. Alongside the boys on the sidewalk was a heavy wooden wagon.

"What are you doing?" Bruce directed the question to Tim. "You're not going to harness Red Rover to that thing, are you?"

"Jerry wanted to try it," Tim said, "but it doesn't look like he's going to get very far. Red has ideas of his own. He doesn't want to be a horse."

"I bet he doesn't," Bruce said. "That dog's not much more than a pup, even if he is a big one. His back's not strong enough to take the weight of that wagon."

"Run along and play with your sister, shrimp." Jerry had dropped to his knees and was adjusting the poles that were attached to the sides of the wagon. "Nobody asked for your advice. We're getting along just fine without it."

"You are, huh?" Bruce tried to control the anger that was building inside him. "You've got a beautiful dog there. What do you want to do, cripple him?"

Jerry finished knotting the poles to the rope harness. Then he got slowly to his feet. His face was dark with fury.

"Let's get something straight. This is my dog — *mine*! He belongs to me, and I'll do what I want with him." He turned to the dog and snapped his fingers. "Up, Red! Let's see you go!"

The dog took a tentative step forward. The rope pulled tight against his chest, and he paused, bewildered. He was being ordered ahead and held back at the same time. He wasn't certain what was expected of him.

"Bruce is right, Jerry," Tim said, as he saw the animal's confusion. "This is a game to you, but it isn't one to Red. Let's get him out of this tangle and play something else."

The other two boys, whom Bruce knew only from having seen them at school, had drawn off a few paces, reluctant to become involved in the argument. They were looking at each other uncomfortably as though wishing they were somewhere else.

Jerry snapped his fingers again. "Giddyup, Red! Do you hear me?"

At the sound of his master's voice, the dog cringed and sank down to a crouch between the traces.

"You see?" Bruce said. "He won't even try. He's got enough sense to know he'll hurt himself."

"He'll try, all right, if he knows what's good for him. Come on, guys, help me get him going!" Jerry motioned to the watching boys. "You give him a shove while I get out in front and call him."

Bruce could stand it no longer.

"Leave him alone!" he shouted. "The poor thing's already scared to death! If anybody shoves him anyplace, I'm going to go get my dad!"

"Oh, you are, huh?" Jerry's reaction was quick and violent. Catching Bruce by the shoulder, he gave him a hard shove backward.

Bruce's legs buckled as the edge of the wagon caught him at the back of the knees. An instant later, all breath went out of him as his shoulders struck the floor of the wagon and his head hit the sharp wooden corner.

"Now, that's what our horse has been waiting for — a load to pull!" Jerry gave an excited laugh. "You stay right there, shrimp! You're going to get a ride you'll never forget!"

Raising the end of the leash high above his head, he brought it down with all his strength across the dog's lean haunches. Then, for good measure, he kicked as hard as he could at Red's left flank.

"Cool it, Jerry!" Tim's face was a mask of horror. "What are you trying to do, kill him?"

Leaping forward, he grabbed for the leash, but the interference came too late. Red Rover let out a high-pitched, almost human, scream of fear and pain and threw himself against the harness.

Bruce felt the wagon lurch beneath him and dazedly tried to pull himself to a sitting position.

He was rolling along the sidewalk. The curb loomed ahead. Bruce threw himself over the edge of the wagon and onto the ground, just as the wagon crashed over the curb and into the street.

Free of Bruce's weight, the wagon flew forward, striking the dog's hind legs. This new assault was the final spur to the terrified animal. He plunged frantically out into the middle of the street, dragging the wagon behind him.

It was Tim who saw the car as it rounded the corner.

"Get him back!" he shouted, but by the time the words left his lips it was already too late. With a crash of splintering wood, the front wheel of the car struck the wagon and crushed it into the street.

Red Rover, the rope harness streaming behind him, tore free of the wreckage and kept running. A moment later, the morning sunlight caught the sheen of his red coat at the end of the street, and then he was gone.

CHAPTER SIX

Sundays in Elmwood were far from Bruce's favorite days. Except for the fact that there was no cleaning to do, they were almost as bad as Saturdays.

It wasn't that he minded going to services. Church had been part of Sunday for as far back as he could remember. It was just that, back in Albuquerque, church had been the beginning of the day, like an introduction. The family had gotten up early and gone and come home again, with the rest of Sunday still ahead of them waiting to be used.

In Elmwood, church and preparing for it consumed most of the day. Aunt Alice liked to rise late, so breakfast didn't start until the middle of the morning. Then, there was getting ready, which was a stressful experience. Because there were so many of them in such a small amount of space, there weren't enough closets and bureaus, and people were seldom able to find the things they needed.

"I'll sure be glad to get into our own place," Bruce grumbled as he plowed through the pile of laundry stacked in the sewing room closet. His own bed was the sofa in the den, and he was supposed to keep his clothes in the same chest of drawers as his sister. "You've got those drawers so crammed with your writing junk there's no room for anything. Why don't you throw out some of those notebooks when you're through with them?"

"Those poems may be valuable someday," Andi said practically. "Imagine if Shakespeare had saved the things he wrote when he was ten!"

"You can't compare yourself to Shakespeare," Bruce said. "He was a genius. He sold every single thing he wrote, and you can't sell a thing."

"I may sell something this week," Andi said pleasantly. "I mailed a poem to *Ladies' Home Journal* two whole weeks ago, and they haven't sent it back. Besides, how do you know that Shakespeare sold everything? He probably just didn't let people know when he didn't."

Andi was in an unusually sunny mood. She had slipped over to the hotel early that morning to give

Friday a bath and her breakfast and was anticipating another long visit with the puppies — which she had named Tom, Dick, and Hairy — in the late afternoon. There had been sweet rolls for breakfast, and she had managed to grab two of them, and it was quite possible that she might become a famous author with the arrival of tomorrow's mail.

In contrast to such cheeriness, Bruce's mood grew darker and darker. He could not find a clean shirt, and his good shoes were missing, and the resulting search took so much time that they were all late to church. Then it turned out to be Communion Sunday, which took an extra half hour, and afterward Aunt Alice ran into some friends and had spent at least twenty minutes chatting with them. By the time they were home and at the dinner table, the whole day seemed to have dissolved with nothing to show for it.

Actually, these new irritations were only partly responsible for Bruce's depression. It had started yesterday with his battle with Jerry. Every time he thought back to the boy's cocky grin and his own undignified ride in the wagon and the sight of the frightened dog cringing between the traces, anger rose within him until it nearly choked him.

"That creep shouldn't be allowed to own a pet," he told Andi afterward. "You should have seen him after that car hit the wagon. Red Rover could have been killed, but that didn't worry him. He was mad because his wagon was broken and the driver of the car wouldn't pay for it."

"He's the meanest person I know," Andi had agreed readily.

Still, she hadn't been as upset as she should have been.

"How old are puppies when their eyes open?" she had asked a moment later, and Bruce had been disgusted. What use was a sister with a temper if she didn't lose it about things that were important?

Sunday dinner was finally reaching its end when the phone rang. Aunt Alice rushed to answer it. A few moments later she returned to the table, shaking her white head regretfully.

"The saddest thing has happened," she said. "That was Mrs. Gordon on the phone. She called to tell us that Jerry's dog is missing."

"That big red setter?" Mr. Walker looked up in surprise. "Why, I thought I saw the kids out playing with him yesterday."

"They're afraid the dog may have been stolen,"

Aunt Alice said. "He's quite valuable, you know. Either that or he's run off somewhere. Children, be sure to keep your eyes open for him when you're outside playing."

"If he's run off, he'll be back," Mr. Walker said. "When a pet gets hungry enough, it comes home."

"I hope he doesn't," Bruce said. "I hope he finds himself another home and never shows up around here again."

"Why, Bruce!" His mother turned to him in amazement. "What a terrible thing to say!"

"I can't believe that of our sweet, kind Bruce!" Aunt Alice looked shocked. "Even if you and Jerry have had a spat, dear, you can't wish for something awful like that. Why, think how heartbroken he must be!"

"If he is," Bruce said, "it's because he's lost something that belongs to him, not because he loves Red Rover. He's so used to having everything just how he wants it that he's mad now because it isn't, that's all."

"Bruce, dear —" His mother caught his eye and raised her brows in a little that's-enough-for-now expression.

"May I be excused, please?" Andi asked.

From her face, Bruce could tell that she had not been listening to any part of the conversation. Her whole mind was at the dog hotel with Friday and the puppies.

"Don't bother with clearing or anything," she said sweetly to her mother and Aunt Alice. "I'll do the cleanup."

"Why, Andi, that's three dinners in a row!" Aunt Alice beamed at her great-niece. "What a thoughtful little girl you are! Your mother is so lucky to have such a helper in the family!"

"Yes, indeed," Mrs. Walker said doubtfully. Both her parents were looking at Andi in a funny way.

"I like to help," Andi said. "It's practice for when I'm grown and have my own kitchen." Hopping up from her chair, she began to carry out the dishes.

When Bruce came out to the kitchen a few minutes later, Andi was standing with her back toward him. When the door swung open, she bent over to conceal what she was doing.

"It's just me." Bruce let the door swing closed behind him. "What are you trying to do, make the whole family suspicious? All that 'I like to help' business. Couldn't you see Mom looking at you like she thought you were sick or something?"

"Well, it wasn't all a lie," Andi said defensively. "I *will* have a kitchen of my own someday. Of course, by that time I expect to be rich and famous enough to hire maids to take care of it."

"You'd better start wishing yourself rich right now," Bruce said. "At least, rich enough to buy some dog food. You know you're not going to get away with this for long." He gestured toward the bowl of chicken and vegetables that his sister had been filling when he entered.

"I don't know about that. It's worked pretty well so far. Mom thinks Aunt Alice eats up the leftovers for a bedtime snack, and Aunt Alice thinks Dad does, and they're all too polite to say anything." Andi picked up the bowl from the counter. "I'm going to take this over to Friday."

"Load the dishwasher first," Bruce advised her. "Somebody might come out here to check on how you're doing."

"I'm just going to be a minute!" Andi opened the door and, holding the bowl carefully so the gravy wouldn't spill, started out into the yard.

A moment later she was back.

"Bruce, he's out there!"

"Who?" Bruce regarded her blankly.

"Jerry Gordon's dog! He's over in the corner of the yard. He's dug a hole under a bush and he's lying in it, and he looks awful."

"Red's *here*!" Pushing past his sister, Bruce hurried out the door.

There was a dog, all right, under a bush as Andi had described. For a moment he could not believe that the dog was Red Rover.

Gone was the shiny coat, the proud lift of the head, the gaily waving plume of a tail. This dog's hair was dull and lusterless, matted with mud and burrs. His tail was curled under him, and his head was pressed against the ground. He did not lift it when Bruce approached or even when he spoke to him. A frayed rope circled his neck.

"It's the harness. He must have tried rubbing it off and got it pushed up around his neck." Bruce knelt on the ground and began to work on the knot. It was like a lump of steel beneath his fingers. The rope itself was so tight that he could not get so much as a fingernail beneath it.

Andi, who had been watching in horror, ran back to the kitchen. When she returned, she was carrying a paring knife.

"Will this help? Maybe you can cut it."

"I hope I can do that without cutting Red." Bruce took the knife and began sawing nervously against the thinnest part of the rope.

The dog slumped beside him, too miserable to care what was being done to him. When the rope gave way at last, he drew a long rasping breath and looked up gratefully into Bruce's face, but still he didn't try to move.

"He could have been strangled." Bruce ran his fingers gently along the dog's throat. There was a raw, hairless circle where the rope had cut into the tender skin. "He couldn't have lived that way much longer. If you hadn't found him and we hadn't gotten that rope off, he would have died."

"Right next door to his own home!" Andi's voice was low and shaken. "He'd rather dig a hole and die in it than go back to Jerry. Oh, Bruce, imagine how scared he must be of him if he would do that!"

"Don't worry, old fellow." Bruce caressed the drooping head. "I'll take care of you. Nobody's ever going to hurt you again."

"But if we take him back —" Andi began.

"We're not going to," Bruce said quietly. "We've got a new tenant for our hotel."

CHAPTER SEVEN

Getting Red Rover to follow them was not difficult. The big dog seemed to realize that Bruce was his new master. All he had to say was, "Come, Red," and the poor animal struggled to his feet and allowed himself to be led through the backyard of the house next door and across the vacant lot to the dog hotel. The problem came with getting him through the window.

"We'll never make it," Andi said, studying the distance from the ground to the sill and then turning to evaluate the size of the dog. "He's too heavy to lift that high. Do you suppose we could get him to jump?"

"Not in the condition he's in now," Bruce said. "The poor thing can hardly even walk. We'll have to try lifting him. There's no other way."

A voice spoke from behind them. "Why don't you rig a ramp?"

Bruce froze. Then he turned slowly to face the speaker.

"What are you doing here?" he asked in a low, tight voice.

Tim Kelly regarded him calmly.

"Looking for you. I saw you crossing the lot, but I couldn't catch up with you."

He paused and then repeated his original statement. "You could put up a ramp. We've got some old lumber over at my house if you want to use that. All it would take would be a couple of boards propped against the sill."

"You're a spy!" Andi burst out furiously. "I've seen you with Jerry! You're one of his gang, and you're going to run back and tell him we have Red Rover."

"That's crazy," Tim said. "If I was going to do that, would I be offering you boards for a ramp?"

"What's the deal?" A little color was beginning to come back into Bruce's face. "Why do you want to help us hide Red?"

"Do you think I want Jerry to get another crack

at him?" Tim asked. "I was in on that scene yesterday, remember? What do you think I am, some kind of monster? I wouldn't send any animal back to that."

"I thought you wanted to be part of the gang," Bruce said. "You don't want to be a loner, do you? You told me you didn't."

"I wouldn't have to be, would I?" Tim said slowly. "I mean — well, one friend, the right kind of friend — is worth more than being part of a mob of guys following along behind a dictator like Jerry. Anyway, that's the way it's beginning to seem to me." His blue eyes were questioning. "How about you?"

Bruce nodded soberly, but inside he felt like cheering.

"It's *always* seemed like that to me," he said.

The boys stood silent a moment, a little embarrassed by the sudden change in their relationship.

Then Tim grinned. "Okay, that's settled. Now, how about we go over to my house and get those boards?"

"Wait a minute," Andi broke in cautiously. "Before you can be part of the hotel staff, you've got to promise on your honor that you won't tell anybody. Not just about Red, but about Friday, too. And Tom and Dick and Hairy."

"Tom, Dick, and Hairy?" Tim looked bewildered. "Who are they? Who's Friday?"

"They're the rest of the dogs," Andi explained. "They have the pink bedroom. I think we should give Red the family room. That way he'll have more space to move around in when he starts feeling better."

"You mean you've got four dogs in there already!" Tim exclaimed incredulously.

"You have to promise," Andi persisted.

"Of course he promises," Bruce said. "Now, you stay here and keep an eye on Red, while Tim and I get the stuff for the ramp."

Tim's house turned out to be the gray one with the yard full of swings and bicycles across the street from Aunt Alice's. The lumber he had spoken about was stacked along the side of the house.

As they selected the boards they would need, Bruce noticed several round, freckled faces, much like Tim's, gazing down at them from an upstairs window.

"Those are my sisters," Tim said. "I told you how nothing over here is ever private. They'll think we're taking the boards over to Jerry's. He's been talking about wanting to use them to build a clubhouse."

"Well, Jerry will know that's not where we're taking them," Bruce said, glancing worriedly in the direction of the Gordons' house. There was no way to get the boards across the street except to carry them openly. Although no one was in evidence, he could not help the uncomfortable feeling that Jerry was somewhere peering at them. "Which is his window?"

"It's the ground-level window on the side facing your aunt's house," Tim told him. "That's where he has his bedroom. Actually he's got the entire base-ment all to himself. He's got a pool table and a big-screen TV and a kind of gym setup for working out. All he has to do is ask for something and his parents get it for him."

"Let's carry the boards down the driveway into our backyard," Bruce suggested. "That way, if Jerry's watching, he'll think we're going to build something back there. Then we can cut over through the yard next door and across the lot to the hotel."

As they were crossing the yard, Mrs. Walker opened the back door and called out to them.

"Bruce, did you find your sister?"

"She's — well, she's right around here," Bruce said awkwardly. "I just saw her a minute ago."

"I want you to tell her to come home immediately," his mother said in an exasperated voice. "She said she would do the kitchen, and she hasn't even rinsed off the plates. Aunt Alice gets terribly upset when things are left a mess."

Andi was sitting in the grass in the yard behind the hotel. She had Red Rover's head in her lap and was gently stroking his ears.

"You don't have to tell me — I heard her," she said, when Bruce and Tim came up to her. "She sure was yelling loud. Mom never used to yell that way."

"You'd better get over there," Bruce said. "You did say you'd do the cleanup."

"I didn't say when I'd do it," Andi said. "At home Mom never minded if we let the dishes sit for a while before we loaded the dishwasher. Why should it matter so much here?"

"Because it does, that's all." Bruce lowered his end of the boards to the ground. "How do you want to do this, Tim?"

"Simple." Tim lifted the ends he was holding and leaned them against the window ledge. Side by side, they became a slanted bridge between the window and the ground. "Now comes the tough part — getting Red to walk up it."

"I'll go inside and call him," Bruce said.

"That won't work. He doesn't come when he's called. I've seen Jerry call him lots of times, and he just cowers and pretends he doesn't hear."

"He'll come to me," Bruce said with certainty.

Walking to the top of the ramp, he turned to face the dog. "Here, Red!" he called softly. "Come up here with me!"

Without an instant's hesitation, Red Rover lifted his head from Andi's lap and got stiffly to his feet. Crossing to the ramp, he staggered up it until he reached Bruce.

"See!" Bruce's voice was triumphant as he gently eased the big dog through the window. A moment later both were inside the house.

"He's picked you for his master, that's for sure," Tim said, when he and Andi had joined Bruce inside. He glanced about with interest. "Where are the rest of your boarders?"

"In the front bedroom." Andi darted ahead to lead the way down the hall. "Friday just loves it. It's so sunny and pretty. Of course, Red is a man's dog — he'll like the family room. It's all wood paneled."

Friday's room, when the door was thrown open, was as much of a surprise to Bruce as it was to Tim. He had not been in it himself since they had settled the dogs in, and though he knew that Andi had been spending all of her free time here, he had not guessed the extent of her activities.

The room shone! Gone were the dust and the cobwebs that had collected during the long period when the house had stood empty. For a girl who did not like housework, Andi had swept and scrubbed until the floor and woodwork gleamed. The glass of the windows had been cleaned so that the sunlight flooded through, bringing the pink-papered walls to vibrant life.

But this was not all. A pink throw rug lay across the bare boards of the floor. Pink rosebud curtains hung at the side window. A bed, fashioned from a clothes basket, sat in the corner of the room, and, inside it, a fluffy white dog and three puppies lay, curled in luxurious comfort, on a pillow that said "Bone Sweet Bone."

"That's not Friday!" Bruce exclaimed. "Friday's brown!"

"The brown came off," Andi said. "That was just dirt. I washed her with Snow White Shampoo for Senior Citizens, and now her hair's the exact same color as Aunt Alice's."

"But this *room*!" Bruce gestured in amazement at the transformation. "Where did you get all the stuff to make it look like this?"

"Different places." Andi looked smug. "I found the rug up in Aunt Alice's attic. It was just lying there, all rolled up in a corner. The basket was down in the basement. It had old magazines in it."

"How about the curtains?" Bruce stepped closer to examine them more critically. "This isn't old cast-off stuff. This is brand-new material. It hasn't even been hemmed. And that pillow is just like the one Bebe had at home."

"Nobody was using the material." Andi began to look uncomfortable. "It was in the sewing closet. And it *is* Bebe's pillow. I brought it with me to remember her by. I didn't think she'd mind my lending it to Friday."

"She probably wouldn't," Bruce said. "But that material is not yours. Aunt Alice must have bought it for some reason. That's stealing, Andi! You can't take material that somebody paid good money for and cut it up for fun."

"It wasn't for fun," Andi said. "It was for Friday. She's a new mother. She needs to have pretty things around her. Besides, Aunt Alice was never going to make anything out of that. I'm sure she wasn't. She hasn't sewed a single thing since we've been living with her."

"How could she when you're sleeping in the sewing room?" Bruce reminded her. "It can't be the greatest thing for the old lady, having a family land on top of her like this. I bet she's counting the days until she can have her house to herself again and sew like crazy."

"Oh, I don't think so," Andi said decidedly. "I bet she got that material on sale without having any use for it. She's probably been looking at it ever since, just wishing it wasn't there."

"Why did you use it on just one window?" Tim asked her.

"Because that window's on the side of the house where the bushes are. If I'd done the front one, people could have seen the curtains from the street." Andi turned pleadingly to her brother. "You do think they look nice, don't you, Bruce?"

"It's not a question of whether they look nice," Bruce said. "The thing is, you've cut up something that doesn't belong to you. You're going to have to replace that material, Andi. You can't just *take* things, even for Friday."

"You took Red," Andi muttered. "That's stealing too, isn't it? I bet a dog like Red Rover costs a lot more than some old cloth."

"That's different," Bruce said defensively. "I took Red for his own sake."

He paused as the logical part of his mind fought with his feelings. Red Rover was a valuable dog, of that there was no question. Mr. Gordon undoubtedly had paid a good price for him when he bought him for Jerry.

"I'll pay them," he said now, after a moment of consideration. "I'll find out how much a good Irish setter costs, and I'll save up the money and pay it. I'll leave it in an envelope in the Gordons' mailbox."

"It looks like this hotel is getting to be an expensive operation," Tim remarked. "What about food? How are you paying for that?"

"I've been taking table scraps," Andi said. "Bruce thinks that won't work much longer."

"It sure won't after today," Bruce said. "Not after the way you copped out on cleaning the kitchen. From now on you're going to have Mom or Aunt Alice standing over you every time you pick up a dish towel."

"I've seen how Red Rover eats," Tim said. "You'll never take care of him with table scraps. It's going to have to be dog food, and plenty of it. I guess we'll just have to go to work and start earning."

"*We?*" Bruce said. "This isn't your responsibility. It's Andi and I who got ourselves into the hotel business."

"Well, I'd like to be a partner," Tim said. "That is, if you want me. I've never had a dog of my own. This way I can be part owner of five of them."

CHAPTER EIGHT

Having Tim Kelly as part of the hotel staff was nice for Bruce, but it took Andi only a short time to discover that she did not like it at all.

"I wish he had never stuck his nose in," she grumbled.

"You're nuts," Bruce told her. "Tim's cool. Look how much he's helping us! We never could have managed to keep Red in dog food if Tim hadn't found him and me after-school jobs."

"Friday doesn't like him," Andi said. "She knows he isn't used to dogs. It upsets her to have him tramping in to look at her puppies."

This was completely untrue, and both of them knew it. Friday was a proud mother and delighted to show off her puppies to anyone, including Red Rover. The thing Andi really resented was the fact that she no longer was able to run things exactly as she wanted. Until now, she and Bruce had been equal partners, with Andi actually holding the position of manager. Now suddenly everything seemed to have gone out of her control.

"Tim and I are earning the money to run this place," Bruce said. "It's up to us to decide what we're going to do with it."

The two boys were working every afternoon and on Saturdays, raking yards around the neighborhood. Out of their earnings they had purchased a whole case of dog food and a brush and comb for Red and some salve for the injured area around his neck. They were setting the rest of the money aside in a special fund to be used to purchase Red Rover.

"You might spend some of it on Friday," Andi said irritably. "There are so many things she needs — her own brush, for instance, and a collar and rubber bones and things for the puppies."

"Friday ought to feel lucky just to be getting some of Red's food," Bruce said. "Remember, you've still got to pay Aunt Alice for the material you took. You haven't put aside any money for that, not even your allowance."

"I couldn't," Andi said, bristling. "I borrowed

against it last month to buy postage stamps, and then there was a movie — no, two movies — that I *had* to see. And Mom caught me when I was returning Aunt Alice's shampoo, and the tube was almost empty, so she made me replace it —"

"That's okay," Tim said soothingly. "Girls don't know anything about earning money. My sisters never earned a dime in their lives."

The superior tone of his voice infuriated Andi even more than Bruce's statements, and the worst of it was that she couldn't think of a way to respond. It was true that she had never earned money, and with her mother irritated at her and Aunt Alice no longer so certain that she was a "dear, helpful little girl," it didn't look as though she was going to be offered many opportunities to do so.

"I'm reaching the end of my patience," Mrs. Walker had told her in the firmest voice Andi had ever heard her mother use. "Back in Albuquerque we lived in a very casual way, but here we are living in somebody else's home. It's hard when there are so many people in a small house, and you have to do your share."

"Aunt Alice is a picky old maid," Andi said irritably. "All she thinks about is dust, dust, dust.

She's boring and gushy, and I wish we were living in a tent."

"She is not an old maid," Mrs. Walker said. "She was married many happy years to your father's uncle Peter. If she seems 'gushy' to you, it's because she isn't used to children. She never had any of her own, and she doesn't know how to talk to them."

"What's so hard about talking to children?" Andi demanded. "Children are human beings."

"So are grown-ups," her mother said quietly. "If you were to open that stubborn mind of yours a little, you might let yourself discover it. Very few people are boring when you really get to know them."

Andi started to fire back an answer and then, seeing the stressed-out expression on her mother's face, decided against it. Mrs. Walker was no longer nearing the end of her patience — she had already reached it.

Aside from the fact that she was at odds with almost everyone in her family, Andi had another reason for being cross and irritable. Her poem had come back from *Ladies' Home Journal.* She had been very hopeful about that poem. It had been called "Death Owns a Ship" and was the most dramatic thing she had ever written, and the magazine had kept it for three whole weeks.

Toward the end of that time she had become quite certain that they had decided to buy it and were trying to make up their minds about how much to pay her. Every day she had rushed home from school to see if her check had arrived. At night, when she lay in bed at the edge of sleep, she had visualized herself strolling along the sidewalk past the yards where Bruce and Tim were slaving away with their rakes, with Friday and the puppies marching proudly ahead of her, each with a diamond-studded leash attached to an emerald-studded collar.

It had been a terrible disappointment to walk into the house one day and find an envelope waiting for her on the hall table with her poem and a form rejection slip inside. At the bottom of the form there was a handwritten note: *We're sorry we can't use this in an upcoming issue, but your writing shows promise. Do try us again when you are older.*

Older! Andi thought. She would be eleven the first of December. That was less than two months away.

"What's the matter, Andi?" her father had asked her at dinner that night. "You're so quiet.

You must be off in space somewhere, composing a new poem."

Andi drew a long breath and made her announcement.

"No," she said. "I'm not. I've decided not to be a famous writer. In fact, I'm never going to write a poem again."

There was a moment of total silence. Everyone at the table turned to stare at her. Even Aunt Alice stopped talking.

"Why, Andi," Mrs. Walker said finally, "you've always loved writing! How can you simply decide to stop?"

"I've changed my mind," Andi said. She did not want to talk about it any further because she was afraid she might cry. She had been so sure that she would become famous within the time limit that she had set for herself. "I'm going to be something more interesting like a — a — helicopter pilot or maybe a ballet dancer."

"You're not graceful enough to be a dancer," Bruce said. "You can't be a pilot either because you can't stand heights. You wouldn't even look at the pictures I took of the Grand Canyon because you said they made you dizzy."

"Then I'll be a teacher like Mom," snapped Andi, blinking back tears. "Or like Mom *used to be*, before she had to quit work."

The thought of prickly Andi patiently teaching school was so inconceivable that no one could think of a single comment, and the rest of the meal took place at a very quiet table.

The next day at school the subject came up all over again. This time it came from Miss Crosno, Andi's teacher.

"Who was it," she asked, "who turned in a poem along with the English compositions this week? There isn't a name on it, and I don't recognize the handwriting." When no one in the class raised a hand, she continued, "It's called 'Bebe.' It's about a child who loses her dog."

"Oh!" Andi was so startled that she spoke before she could stop herself. "That's mine, but I didn't mean to turn it in. I guess I just got an extra paper mixed in with the composition sheets in the notebook."

"I'm glad I got to see it," Miss Crosno said. "It's a very nice poem with a great deal of feeling. Would you like to come up front, Andi, and read it to the class?"

"No, thank you," Andi said.

Then, because this sounded rude even to her own ears and, after all, Miss Crosno would be the one who would be making out report cards, she added, "I never read my poems to anybody but my family. If they're not good enough to be published, they're not good enough for people to have to listen to."

"Do you submit your poems to magazines?" Miss Crosno asked. "Which ones do you send them to?"

"The ones on Mom's coffee table," Andi said. "But I don't any longer. I've done it for two years now and used up about a million envelopes and stamps, and it hasn't gotten me anywhere, and I think that's enough."

That day at lunchtime, when Andi was unloading her tray at the corner table in the cafeteria where she usually sat and read, she was surprised to find another tray suddenly placed beside her own.

"Is it okay if I sit here?" Debbie Austin asked her.

Debbie had not tried to speak to her since asking her to play double jump rope in the school yard, and Andi could not imagine why she was doing so now.

"Sit wherever you want," she said.

Debbie was unloading her tray and did not seem to notice the ungraciousness.

"I had to talk to you," she said, "after this morning and what Miss Crosno said about your poem. Before, I thought you were just unfriendly, but I didn't know you were a poet. That makes it different. I mean, lots of poets don't play jump rope and things."

"I do play jump rope," Andi said. "I didn't know that's what you meant by 'Double Trouble.'"

"Why didn't you say so?" Debbie sat down across from her and regarded her solemnly. "The thing I wanted to tell you is — now don't repeat this to anybody, I don't want the other kids to think I'm a nerd — but I write poetry, too."

"You do!" Andi said. It never had occurred to her that other girls ever wrote poetry.

"I have a whole notebook of poems at home," Debbie said. "I keep it hidden under my bed so my brother won't see it. He says only dweebs write poetry."

"That's not so," Andi said. "It takes very bright people to be poets. Think of Shakespeare and people like that. Besides, you're not a dweeb. You're very popular."

"Well, yes," Debbie admitted. "I guess you could say that. Still, I don't have anybody I can talk to — I mean *really* talk to — about things that matter. Most of my friends feel just like my brother does. I don't want people to think I'm weird."

"I personally don't mind it," Andi said. Then she paused and added more honestly, "Well, yes, I do mind it some. It would be nice to be popular. Maybe I will be, now that I've stopped writing."

"What do you write about?" Debbie asked. "I mean, what did you write about back when you were a poet?"

"Sad things mostly," Andi said. "My last poem, the one I sent to the *Journal*, was about shipwrecks." She drew a deep breath and quoted:

> *Death owns a ship that roams the seas,*
> *A ship that the boldest seamen dread.*
> *It's made of the air and the clouds and*
> *   the storm,*
> *And its cargo is the dead.*

"Wow!" Debbie's eyes widened in admiration, and she gave a shudder. "That's the goriest thing

I've ever heard. I don't see how any magazine could help but buy it!"

"Well, they didn't," Andi said. "I'm practically eleven now, and I can't be spending all my time on something that isn't bringing any success. Especially now when I've got to start finding ways to earn money, because Friday isn't getting half the nice things Red Rover is getting and —"

She stopped herself in horror and clamped her mouth closed tight.

"Who is Friday?" Debbie asked, exactly as Tim had the first day he came to the hotel.

Perhaps it was the thought of Tim's question that did it, Tim's question and the memory of Bruce's answer, *"Of course he won't tell."* What right had Bruce had to decide whether or not Tim could be trusted when she herself had not decided? Why should Bruce be able to pick out a friend and make him a member of the hotel staff when she, Andi, didn't?

Two boys and one girl — it wasn't a fair balance. How could the girl ever hope to have anything her way as long as the boys outnumbered her? But if there were *two* girls —

Thoughtfully, Andi regarded the girl across the table from her. Debbie was certainly not a blabbermouth. If she were, she never would have kept the fact that she was a poet from all of her friends.

"Can you keep a secret?" Andi asked.

"Of course." Debbie's voice dropped to a whisper, and she leaned forward eagerly. "Is it about a poem?"

"No," Andi said. "It's Friday. She's a dog, and Red Rover's a dog, and there are three others who are just puppies. My brother and I are running a hotel for them."

"A hotel!" Debbie exclaimed. "You mean you take homeless dogs off the streets and give them a place to stay?"

"Something like that," Andi said.

Debbie's face was aglow with excitement. "That's awesome! Do you suppose — oh, Andi, does the hotel have an extra room for another guest?"

"It has all sorts of rooms," Andi said. "There's a whole second floor. But what other guest are you thinking about?"

"MacTavish," said Debbie.

"Who?" Now it was Andi's turn to look blank.

"That's the black-and-white dog who always hangs around the school grounds. He used to belong to a boy who went to school here, but last summer the boy's family moved and they didn't take MacTavish with them."

Andi was horrified. "You mean they left him here to starve?"

"Oh, he doesn't starve," Debbie said. "All the kids feed him, and he sits outside the cafeteria at lunchtime and the ladies who do the cooking put out scraps for him. The thing is, it's starting to get cold now. What will he do when winter comes and he doesn't have a warm place to go?"

"Isn't there anybody who wants him?" Andi asked. She thought of the careful plans her own family had made to leave Bebe with the Arquettes. How could people possibly get into a car and drive off without making any kind of arrangements to have their pets cared for?

"Couldn't you take him?" she asked.

"If only," Debbie said wistfully. "But my mother has a cat. Fluffy is a very special, blue-ribbon Persian, and she hates dogs. If we got one, Mom is afraid Fluffy might run away."

"Isn't there anyone else who might want him?"

Andi asked the question, but her mind was flying ahead of her. It was moving on wings down the hallway that led from Friday's pink bedroom, past the family room where Red Rover stayed, and up the stairs to the second-floor hall where a whole row of doors opened into unused bedrooms.

I wonder, she thought, *if a black-and-white dog would like blue wallpaper better than green?*

CHAPTER NINE

There was nothing difficult about locating MacTavish. When school was out for the day, Debbie led the way to the back of the cafeteria, and there he was. When she saw him, Andi had the immediate feeling that he was waiting there just for her.

"I wish I could help you get him to the hotel," Debbie said. "I would if I didn't have a Scout meeting."

"I can manage fine," Andi told her. "He isn't so big. I was afraid he might be the size of Red Rover."

Actually, although he was a small dog, MacTavish was heavy, for he had gained a good deal of weight eating sandwich crusts and potato chips and spaghetti left over from school lunches. Andi was panting by the time she got him to the hotel.

Still, it was worth it! Never had she seen a dog so happy! She had decided to give him the blue room, as it had a built-in window seat from which a dog could look out over the backyard, and MacTavish leaped up there at once. From there he jumped to the floor and ran around sniffing, exploring the room from one corner to another. Then he leaped upon Andi. Wagging and licking and wriggling with delight, he burrowed into her arms, making little squeaking sounds of joy.

Hooray! he seemed to be saying. *At last I have a home!*

"You poor thing! Imagine your master going off and leaving you!" Andi hugged the dog hard, ducking her head to keep the busy pink tongue from washing her face. "Just wait until Bruce sees you! Friday's so busy with her puppies, she isn't much company for Red Rover. Bruce will be so glad to have a friend for Red to play with!"

She was wrong about that, however. Bruce was not happy at all.

"Another dog!" He regarded his sister with disbelief. "Andi Walker, you must be crazy! Tim and I are working ourselves to death to take care of the ones we already have."

"He won't eat much," Andi said. "He's already fat. One meal a day should do him just fine."

"Fat dogs eat more than thin ones," Tim volunteered. He and Bruce had stopped by the hotel on their way over to the Kellys' to get their rakes. "It's the same with fat people. Their stomachs stretch, and they have to eat more and more food to fill them up."

"That's not so," Andi contradicted. "Aunt Alice is fat, and she hardly eats anything. Besides, we won't have to buy all the food. Debbie thinks if we ask the ladies at the cafeteria to save the scraps and put them in a bag —"

"Debbie!" Bruce pounced upon the unfamiliar name. "Who's Debbie? Have you been blabbing around about the hotel? I thought we all promised —"

"I haven't been blabbing," Andi said. "I only told Debbie. She's my best friend, just the way Tim is yours."

"What do you mean, your best friend?" Bruce exploded. "I've never even heard of her! If you have a best friend, why haven't you ever had her over?"

"I am going to have her over tomorrow," Andi told him. "She's going to help me with the hotel housework. Now that we have six guests, there's too much work for one person to do alone. You boys never help."

"Never help!" Bruce was so angry that it was all he could do to keep from grabbing his sister and shaking her until her teeth rattled. "What do you call all those hours Tim and I put in after school and on weekends raking leaves?"

"That's not the same thing," Andi said. "It really isn't, Bruce. I feed them and clean up after them."

Then, because it seemed very likely that her brother might be about to hit her, she snatched MacTavish into her arms and ran out of the room.

"You shouldn't let her get to you like that," Tim remarked later, as the boys collected their rakes from the Kellys' garage. "She's just acting like a girl. My sisters are the same way sometimes."

"I know," Bruce said wearily. "I never used to get so mad at her. It's just today — bringing home that blasted dog without even checking with us first —"

"He seems like a nice dog," Tim said. "Those black ears and white face make him look like a clown. Those pups of Friday's are going to be ready to leave her in another week or so anyway."

"That's true. They're already beginning to eat solid food." Bruce brightened slightly. "If we get rid of them, that will cut things down by half."

Even so, he had far from a joyful expression on his face as he and Tim set off down the street toward their afternoon job.

Bruce was exhausted. He had always been a boy who enjoyed having time to himself — time for reading, for playing with other boys, for puttering around with his photography. Now suddenly there was no time at all. When he was not in school, he was working, and when he wasn't working, he was trying to study — *trying* because by the time dinner was over and he was ready to settle down to his books, he was usually so sleepy that he could not keep the words on the page from running together.

It showed in his grades.

"I don't understand what's happened," his father said the day report cards came out. "You've always been an A student. Where did these Bs and Cs come from all of a sudden?"

"Maybe the schools in Elmwood are more advanced than the ones out West," Aunt Alice suggested. "Perhaps they grade harder here."

"In that case, Bruce should be working harder."

Mr. Walker had no patience with average marks. He knew that both Bruce and Andi were bright children, and he had always expected them to stay at the top of their classes. The fact that his wife was a teacher only enhanced those expectations.

"I know I should, Dad." Bruce struggled to stifle a yawn. "I'll get at that math tonight."

"You look as though you could fall asleep right here at the table," his mother said worriedly. "Can't you do some of your studying in the afternoon?" She turned to her husband. "He and Andi both go out to play right after school every day. They're out all afternoon, *every* afternoon."

"I'm not tired. It's only eight o'clock." Bruce forced his eyes wide. The last thing he wanted was to be forbidden to spend his afternoons away from the house. "I'm just sort of groggy from eating so much. I'll wake right up as soon as I get going on that math."

But the math problems, when he opened his book to them, seemed to be written in a foreign language. There was no sense to any of them, even the simple ones. Numbers danced before Bruce's eyes like black dots, shifting and whirling about against the white page. By the time twenty minutes had passed, he was fast asleep with his face buried in the book.

There was good reason for Bruce's weariness. Not only was he doing more outdoor physical work than he ever had done in his life, but he was getting up at five o'clock every morning. It was at this time of day that Red Rover had his exercise.

Exercising the small dogs was no problem. They could romp in the yard behind the hotel where the bushes were a protective screen cutting them off from the street. Every afternoon Andi took them outdoors for playtime, and they went out again after dinner.

Red Rover presented a different problem. He could not be satisfied with chasing a ball around a tiny restricted area. Red was a big dog, a dog bred for running. As his wounds began to heal and his health and good spirits returned, so too did his energy. He roamed restlessly around the hotel, scratching at the doors and propping his big paws on the sills to gaze wistfully out windows. Sometimes he barked.

"That's not good," Tim said worriedly. "Even with the house set back like it is, sounds carry. Somebody might be walking past and hear him."

"I can run him at night." It was Bruce who had come up with the idea. "That way there wouldn't be any chance of Jerry and his parents seeing him. I sleep on the couch in the den. Everybody else in the family sleeps upstairs. I could sneak out when they're all asleep and nobody would know the difference."

"I wish I could help you," Tim said. "I feel like a cop-out not doing my part, but my bedroom is next to the girls'. There's always one of them hopping up and down for water or something. They'd catch me first thing and go tattling off to our parents."

"That's okay," Bruce said. "I don't mind doing it myself. I'll set my alarm for two hours earlier than I usually get up and have Red out and back again before it gets light."

The first time he had tried this, the alarm clock had gone off like a fire alarm. The shrill sound had been so shattering in the stillness of the sleeping house that both his parents and Aunt Alice had awakened in terror.

"What was that? Did you hear that? Was it the doorbell?"

"Telephone?"

"Could someone have set off a car alarm?"

"I'm sure it was an air-raid siren!" screamed Aunt Alice. "Do you suppose some foreign country has decided to attack us in the night?"

Lying huddled in his bed with the now-silent clock clutched protectively to his chest, Bruce heard their frantic voices as they rushed through the upstairs hall, pulling on robes, snatching up the phone receiver, and finally running down the stairs to see if someone was at the front door.

After that he kept the alarm clock under his pillow. This muffled the sound, and soon he grew so used to having it there that he began to waken at the first tiny click before the bell even had a chance to ring.

Getting out of bed was the hard part. Once he was into his clothes and out of the house, there was something exhilarating about being up and about before the rest of the world. The sky, still dotted with stars, and the cold, fresh smell of the air filled him with a special kind of excitement.

Raising the ramp against the window ledge, he would hear Red Rover stirring around inside, already awake and eager for his outing.

"Red?"

He never had to speak more than once. The big dog would be upon him, tail thumping excitedly, body quivering with anticipation.

Once they were outside, the world opened before them, theirs alone. It was night when they started off along the deserted streets, but soon the dark shapes of trees began to emerge against the gradually paling sky. Red was like a wild thing in the joy of his freedom, first racing ahead, then loping back to circle Bruce and fly off again in another direction.

Then, in what seemed a matter of minutes, it was morning. The sky lightened in the east, turning from gray to a soft pink. Birds began to twitter in the trees, making drowsy, coming-awake noises. Somewhere a baby cried, the sound surprisingly loud through the stillness.

Then the sun itself appeared, a bright red ball over the treetops, and the whole sky exploded with color. It was so much brighter, so much more thrilling, Bruce thought in wonder, than it ever was in an evening sunset! This was the point at which he turned Red toward home.

As he told Tim, he did not mind those morning outings. It was fun being out alone with Red. It made him feel in a way as though he were the dog's real master.

No matter how much he enjoyed himself, however, the fact remained that each morning he was sacrificing two hours of sleep. The rest of the day seemed to drag on forever. Sitting in class, Bruce would find his head nodding, his eyelids drooping. The sound of the teacher's voice would begin to drone like a lullaby, and before class was half over he would be fighting to stay awake.

Despite his exhaustion, Bruce did make an effort to do more studying. The grades on his first-quarter report card had shocked him as much as they had his father. He was used to being at the top of his class, and to find himself getting Cs where he once had gotten As was an upsetting experience.

Every night after dinner he spread his books out on the table in the den and tried to concentrate. Often he ended up falling asleep on top of them.

It was during one of these times that his mother came in and found him there. She stood gazing down at him worriedly.

"I can't understand it," she said softly. "It isn't even eight-thirty. Can he be sick, I wonder? Maybe

I should make a doctor's appointment and see that he gets a complete checkup." Leaning over, she touched his arm. "Bruce? You'd better go to bed. You're not going to get any studying done tonight."

Bruce mumbled something and turned his face against his outstretched arm.

"Come, honey, I'll help you."

Mrs. Walker put her arm around him and dragged him to his feet. Steering him to the sofa, she helped him onto it. Bruce was so heavily asleep the moment his head touched the pillow that he was not even aware of his mother removing his shoes. She drew a blanket over him and quietly turned out the light.

The next day he awoke to the pale light of early morning. For a moment he lay there wondering what had happened. It had been weeks since he had wakened to anything but total darkness. Sliding his hand under the pillow, he groped for the clock. It wasn't there. Lifting his head, he saw it on the table next to the couch. He had fallen asleep the night before without setting the alarm, and now it was morning.

"Poor Red!" Bruce snapped into a sitting position, shocked wide awake. "He's probably over there, tearing the walls down!"

Grabbing for the shoes that his mother had placed beside the sofa, he hurriedly began to put them on. It was still early. It had to be. The light was dim. He could barely make out the blur of his jacket thrown across the back of the chair by the door. People in Elmwood were not generally early risers. Streets were free of cars until close to seven.

I can still give him a quick run, Bruce thought as he pulled on his jacket. *The Gordons aren't going to be sitting on their lawn to watch the sunrise. We'll just take a fast trek down the street and back again. It won't be much for Red, but it will be better than nothing.*

Heavy fog engulfed him as he left the house. He could hardly see ten feet before him, but by the time he reached the empty lot between the houses, he could hear the short, sharp sounds of impatient barking.

When he reached the hotel, Red Rover was so happy to see him that he nearly knocked him over.

"Simmer down, boy. Calm down." Bruce gave the leaping animal a quick pat. "This is going to be a short one this morning."

When he opened the door at the end of the hall the dog shot past him with the speed of a bullet. Up he went to the back window and down the ramp. By the time Bruce had followed him outside, he was nowhere to be seen.

"Red! Hey, Red, where are you?" Bruce called softly, keeping his voice low. "Red Rover, come on back here!"

Rounding the corner of the house, he crossed the front yard to the sidewalk. He looked up and down the street in both directions. Somewhere ahead of him a streak of red flashed across a yard and disappeared into the mists. Bruce began to run. He reached the yard and stopped.

"Red! Red Rover!" He called more loudly this time.

The fog was heavy, shutting off his view of the end of the street. A garbage truck rattled by. Across the street from him, the door of a house opened, and a woman stuck out her head.

"Here, kitty, kitty, kitty! Come get your breakfast!" Her voice was thin and shrill.

It's later than I thought! Bruce realized. *It's the fog that made everything seem darker.* A feeling of panic came over him. *I've got to get hold of Red! I've got to get him home fast!*

It was impossible to know with any certainty

where the dog had gone. Bruce hurried along the sidewalk, glancing frantically into yards on either side. Every few paces he stopped to call Red's name.

"You looking for somebody?" a voice called to him. A newspaper delivery boy pulled his bicycle to a stop next to the curb.

"Yes. No. I mean, it's not a person." Bruce didn't know how to answer. "I'm looking for a —"

The boy was not listening. His attention was directed toward a side street.

"Look at that, will you!" he exclaimed. "It looks like one of those ghost hounds on television!"

Following his gaze, Bruce saw the outline of a dog against a bank of fog.

"It's not a ghost," he said. "It's —"

"Like a sci-fi movie." The boy leaned forward. "Here he comes!"

Red Rover galloped toward them.

"That's no spirit dog!" the boy cried. "He sure looked like one for a minute, but that's a real animal! Hey, isn't that the setter that's been missing from that house down the street? The one they've posted a reward for?"

"I don't think so," Bruce said quickly as Red shot past them. He was headed for home now. He'd had his run and knew that breakfast awaited him back at the hotel.

"I bet it is," the boy said. "I sure wish I'd thought about that in time to grab him."

"It's not the same dog," Bruce insisted. "I'm sure it's not. That dog used to live next door to me — the one that's lost, I mean. I've seen him close up. This dog here didn't look at all like him."

"Well, I think he did," the boy said. "I deliver papers to that house, so I've seen the setter. There can't be many big dogs like that running loose around the neighborhood."

He turned to Bruce, his eyes narrowing with sudden suspicion. "I bet I know what you've got in mind. You're trying to discourage me so you can claim that reward yourself. Well, it's not going to work, kid!" He grinned triumphantly. "I'm going down to that house right now and telling them I've seen their ghost dog and the reward is *mine*!"

CHAPTER TEN

The day the puppies ate a whole can of dog food and whined for more, Bruce pronounced them old enough to leave their mother.

"You'd better line up some homes for them fast, before they start eating the wallpaper," he told Andi.

Although she had known all along that such a time was inevitable, Andi was heartbroken.

"It's too soon," she mourned to Debbie as they walked to school together. "I never should have taught them to eat out of a dish. If they couldn't do that, Bruce wouldn't make us get rid of them."

"I wish I could take one," Debbie said wistfully. She was spending much of her spare time at the hotel and had become very fond of the puppies.

"That little Hairy is such a darling. I'd much rather have him than Mom's stupid cat."

"It's not fair," Andi said. "If we have to send somebody away, why couldn't it be Red Rover? He eats ten times as much as those tiny puppies. But, no, Red is special, because Bruce and Tim are boys and they like big dogs better than little ones."

Despite her feelings, she kept her promise and posted a notice about the puppies on the school bulletin board. She printed it in the tiniest letters possible in the hope that no one would notice it crammed in among all the other announcements. She soon realized, however, that this had been a bad mistake. The fact that the writing was so small that it could not be read easily made everyone who saw it curious about what it said.

A small group gathered around the board, and other passersby pushed their way in to see what was so interesting. Before long, the hallway in front of the bulletin board was jammed with students struggling to make out the message:

FREE PUPPIES, BROWN AND WHITE

CAN BE DELIVERED TO YOUR HOME

SEE ANDI WALKER, ROOM 207

"Free puppies!" One girl let out a little squeal. "What fun! I wonder if my mother would let me have one."

"It's my brother's birthday next Monday," another girl said. "He'll be seven years old. I bet he'd love to have a puppy."

"My dog was hit by a car a couple of months ago," a boy said sadly. "When that happened I felt like I'd never want another pet. But now — I don't know — when you're used to having a dog around, it gets kind of lonesome without one."

When the bell rang for recess, Andi found four people waiting for her in the hall outside the classroom. The girl with the little brother and the boy whose dog had been run over were definite about wanting puppies. Andi agreed to deliver them the next day. The other girl wanted to know how big they were, and, when Andi told her, she said that she liked small dogs and was almost sure she would take one but would have to check first to get her parents' permission.

The fourth person was from Andi's class, although she didn't know her very well. She was a thin, quiet, brown-haired girl named Tiffany Tinkle. Andi had always thought of Tiffany as a little beige mouse.

Now the mouse spoke.

"I saw your ad on the board," Tiffany said in a wispy voice.

"I guess everybody did," Andi said. As usual, when speaking to someone she did not know well, she heard her voice sounding cold and snippy, even though she did not mean for it to be that way. "I'm sorry, but you're too late to get one. They've already been promised."

"All of them?" Tiffany exclaimed. "Every single one of them? That's incredible! Our dog, Ginger, had five puppies a couple of months ago, and we haven't been able to find homes for any of them. Ginger's a purebred Airedale, but her husband was a bulldog. That's kind of a funny combination."

"All puppies are cute, no matter who their parents are," Andi said. "You're lucky if you *can't* find homes for them. I wish I could keep Friday's puppies and watch them grow up."

"Oh, there's no chance of our keeping them," Tiffany said. "My father says one dog in the family is plenty. If we don't find homes for the pups soon, he's going to drown them."

"He's going to do *what*?" Andi was so horrified that she forgot to be stiff and awkward. She could not believe her ears. "Your father must be a horrid, unfeeling monster!"

"He's very strict," Tiffany agreed, looking more like a mouse than ever. "He was hoping Ginger would have Airedale puppies so we could sell them for a lot of money. When she fell in love with the bulldog next door, Daddy got furious. He says he doesn't want a lot of half-breed mutts around the place."

"He sounds like exactly the sort of man Jerry Gordon will be when he grows up," Andi said. "My dad's strict too, but he'd die before he'd hurt a helpless little puppy. You aren't going to let him do that, are you, Tiffany? Can't you do something?"

"I don't know what," Tiffany said forlornly. "When Daddy makes up his mind, that's that. Do you know anyone who would take a puppy?"

"I've used up all the people I know," Andi said. "What about putting an ad on the bulletin board the way I did? I bet you get homes for all the pups right away."

"Do you really think so?" Tiffany brightened. "That would be wonderful. What should I say?"

"Don't say they're part bulldog," Andi advised

her. "Let people figure that out for themselves. If you have to say anything, you can say they're a large part Airedale."

Tiffany looked doubtful. "They're not, though. They're just *half* Airedale."

"Don't be so picky," Andi said impatiently. "That's a large enough part."

Grabbing Tiffany's hand, she dragged her down the hall to the bulletin board.

This time there was no group standing in front of it. There was just one person, Mr. Strode, the school principal. He had taken down Andi's notice and was holding it close to his eyes, squinting as he struggled to read it without his glasses.

He glanced up as the girls approached him.

"Hello, girls," he said. "Do either of you happen to know who this Andi Walker is?"

If Tiffany had not been with her, Andi might have been tempted to say no. As it was, that wasn't an option.

"I am, sir," she said in a small voice.

"Then you're the one who put this on the board this morning?" Mr. Strode was frowning. His brows drew together across the top of his nose in a straight gray line. "This board is only for notices pertaining to school activities — club meetings, sports events, and things like that."

"I'm sorry," Andi said. "I didn't know. I mean, I didn't really think — "

"No notices of any kind should be posted on this board without my permission," the principal said.

"I'm sorry, sir," Andi said again.

She glanced at Tiffany, who was twisting her hands together nervously. It was obvious that she was not going to say anything.

"Please, sir," Andi said quickly, before she could lose her nerve, "could we have permission to post another notice? I don't need this first one up any longer because all our puppies have been spoken for, but my friend here has five of them and if we don't find homes for them right away, her father is going to drown them."

"That's a sad situation." Mr. Strode's expression softened. For a moment Andi thought he was going to say yes.

Then slowly he shook his head.

"Even in this case," he said regretfully, "I can't let you use the school bulletin board for a personal notice. If I let you do that, in fairness I'd have to let everybody else do the same. Everyone has something he or she would like to advertise. Pretty soon we'd need ten boards to hold all the ads for dogs and cats and gerbils and goldfish."

His statement was reasonable. There was no way to argue with it. Even if there had been, fifth graders couldn't get anywhere arguing with a school principal. Still, to Andi, *nothing* was reasonable if it meant the lives of five puppies.

She worried about them all afternoon. As she turned the pages of her history book, she saw, instead of pictures of United States presidents, five sad little Airedale-bulldog faces.

When she glanced across at Tiffany, bent over her own book, she felt like snatching something up and throwing it at her. How could she just sit there like that and do absolutely nothing?

If they were my puppies, I'd think of some way to save them, Andi told herself bitterly. *If I couldn't find homes for them, I'd hide them and raise them secretly. I'd train them to do tricks, and when they were grown I'd sell them to a circus.*

The more she thought about it, the better the idea seemed to her. Surely the funnier-looking a dog was, the better a circus would like it. The whole idea of a circus was to make people laugh. Training dogs was not too difficult, either. She had trained Bebe to shake hands and roll over and bark when she wanted a treat. It couldn't be much harder to teach more exotic things, such as walking a tightrope and dancing and jumping through hoops.

By the time the final bell rang, Andi was bursting with excitement.

"Tiffany!" she cried, rushing to catch up with her. "Wait a minute! I have an idea."

Tiffany turned hopefully, but once Andi had explained the plan to her, she did not seem enthusiastic.

"I don't know," she said. "I've never trained a dog. Besides, I don't know where I'd hide them."

"Don't worry about little things like that." Andi brushed the problems aside. "I have a place where we can keep them, and I'll help with the training. We'll get a book about teaching animals circus tricks. All you have to do is keep it a secret until they're ready to give a performance."

Debbie, when Andi described her plan to her, did not share her enthusiasm, either.

"Tiffany's an awful baby," she said doubtfully. "It's hard to imagine her keeping a secret if somebody tried to make her tell it."

"I know," Andi said. "I don't like that part of it, either. Still, we have to save those puppies. I haven't even seen them, and I love them already just the way I do Tom and Dick and Hairy."

"I guess you're right," Debbie agreed with a sigh. "We'll just have to take the chance."

When they reached Tiffany's house that afternoon and saw the puppies, they had no doubts that what they were doing was right. The pups were big ones, much larger than Friday's, with shaggy Airedale hair and square bulldog faces, but their stubby tails never stopped wagging. They tumbled and rolled and bounced, falling over their feet to be the first to greet their guests.

"What clowns!" Andi picked up the nearest puppy and hugged it while the rest swarmed about her, yipping their jealousy. "We'll give them the big, green bedroom upstairs next to MacTavish."

"When your father comes home from work tonight, you can tell him you gave the puppies to some classmates," Debbie said firmly to Tiffany.

"But don't you dare say who those classmates are or what they're going to do with them."

Getting the puppies to the hotel was a nightmare. There were so many, and they were so wiggly and squirmy. There was an alley behind Tiffany's house that ran the length of the block, but beyond that there was only the sidewalk. Andi and Debbie each carried two puppies, and Tiffany one. Everybody they passed turned to stare at them.

"Where are you going?" one lady asked. "To a dog show?"

A mother with a baby came by, and the baby squealed, "Tigger! Tigger!" and nearly fell out of his stroller.

"Those aren't tigers, honey," his mother explained to him. "They're doggies. And such a lot of them!"

But the baby kept shrieking, "Tigger! Tigger!" all the way down the street until his mother took him around a corner.

Two little boys passed on bicycles, waving and shouting. The puppies yipped back at them and squirmed with delight. They would have loved to have been able to get down and chase the bikes.

"We're almost there," Debbie panted, as they came to the final block. "Just a little farther and — *oh, no!*"

"What is it?" Andi asked, and turned her head to see what Debbie was looking at.

Now it was her turn to say *"Oh, no!"*

Coming toward them along the sidewalk was Jerry Gordon.

CHAPTER ELEVEN

He was by himself. That was the first thing that Andi noticed. He did not look nearly as imposing when he was alone as he did when he was surrounded by his gang of followers.

Come to think of it, I haven't seen any kids going in or out of his house for quite a while now, she thought suddenly. She did not have time to take the thought further because Jerry had reached them.

"Well, what do we have here?" He stopped in front of them, blocking their way. Surprisingly he seemed almost glad to see them. "What are you doing with those dogs, Andi? Your aunt's allergic to them. She told my father about that when he got me Red Rover."

"They're not my dogs," Andi said, her arms tightening protectively around the puppies. "They belong to Tiffany. We're hunting for homes for

120

them. We're going to knock on doors up and down the street to see if anybody wants them."

The moment she said it, she realized that it was not a bad idea. Why *not* knock on doors and see if anyone wanted a puppy? The fewer there were when they reached the hotel, the less food it would take to raise them.

"They're funny looking," Jerry said. He reached out a finger and poked at one of the puppies. "Nobody with any sense is going to want a mutt like this."

"They are *not* mutts," Andi said furiously. "These are purebred Bulldales! They're the latest breed! All the movie stars have them! They're winning all the prizes at dog shows these days!"

"They are?" Jerry looked skeptical, but there was a flicker of interest in his eyes. "If they're that great, how come you haven't been able to give any of them away?"

"We have," Andi said, glad that Bruce was not there to hear her. "We've given away five of them just since school let out. See, there are only five left where there used to be ten."

"They're really going that fast?" Jerry tried not to show it, but his interest was increasing. He studied the pups carefully. Suddenly he smiled. It was the bright, sweet smile he usually used with grown-ups.

"Well, I guess I'll help you out. I'll take that one," and he pointed to the largest puppy, which was one of the two that Debbie was carrying.

For a moment there was silence. Everyone was too astonished to speak.

Then Andi said explosively, "You certainly will not!"

"Andi!" Tiffany turned to her in bewilderment. "What are you saying? Isn't that what we want — to find the puppies homes?"

"Not with somebody like Jerry Gordon," Andi said. "I wouldn't send a mountain lion to live at the Gordons' house."

"Look here!" Jerry's handsome face flushed with anger. "You just finished telling me these aren't your puppies! They belong to this other girl. I want a dog, and she wants me to have one, and I don't see why you should have anything to say about it."

"Tiffany does *not* want you to have one!" Debbie exclaimed. She turned to Tiffany. "Don't you dare give him a puppy! Jerry tortured his last dog until it ran away. Bruce and Tim told me all about it."

"He didn't run away," Jerry said. "Somebody stole him. That somebody lives right in this neighborhood, too! The kid who delivers our newspaper saw Red the other morning. He said he looked like a ghost running through the fog, but he recognized him and was sure it was Red Rover."

"You beat that poor dog and tied a rope around his neck that almost strangled him!" Andi cried. "It's a wonder he didn't break his back trying to run with that wagon behind him. In fact—" She forced herself to stop before she said too much.

Jerry was watching her intently.

"In fact, what?" he asked. "You seem to know a lot about my dog. What 'fact' were you going to tell me?"

"In fact—" Andi realized that she had gone too far. Frantically she searched her mind for some way to end her sentence. "In fact," she said slowly, "I bet you *did* break his back. I bet he ran off someplace and dug a hole and climbed into it and died. I bet it *was* a ghost dog that newspaper kid saw."

"That's crazy." Clearly Jerry had not been expecting anything like that. "Dogs can't be ghosts. They don't have souls."

"How do you know they don't?" Andi shot back

at him. "A dog like Red Rover has more of a soul than you'll ever have. I bet he's a ghost, and I hope he comes through your walls at night and haunts you!"

With that, she clutched the two puppies she was holding tightly against her chest and marched around Jerry and on down the street. At the corner the other two girls caught up with her. Debbie grabbed her arm and squeezed it triumphantly.

"Andi, you were great! How do you ever come up with such things? You should have seen his face after you walked off. He turned white as a sheet."

"How could you lie like that?" Tiffany asked in a shocked voice. "You made all that up, Andi Walker, about there being ten puppies and all the movie stars having them — none of it was true!"

"I know," Andi said. "Now, come on, let's cut through our side yard and go to the hotel from the back so Jerry won't see us."

When the girls reached the hotel, Bruce and Tim were there already. Tim saw them first. He was coming down the stairs, carrying MacTavish's water bowl.

"Where have you been so long?" he asked irritably. "School's been out for an hour. Bruce and I have had to do all your housework, cleaning up after the dogs and filling the water bowls and —"

He broke off suddenly when he saw what Andi was carrying.

"Yikes! Bruce, come see what your crazy sister has brought with her!"

"It better not be another dog!" Bruce came in from the den with Red Rover at his heels. "One more bottomless pit like MacTavish to feed and we'll be broke!" His eyes widened in disbelief. "I don't believe it! *Five of them!* And who's *that*?"

"She's Tiffany Tinkle," Andi said. "Tiffany, this is my brother, Bruce, and that's Tim Kelly."

"You know we agreed not to bring in any more partners," Bruce said. "And five new dogs —"

"I've found homes for Friday's puppies," Andi said quickly. "So, really, it's just two more dogs than before, not five, and we have grand plans for these. We're going to train them for the circus."

"They look like circus dogs, that's for sure." Tim took Tiffany's puppy from her and set it on the floor. "Here, Red, come meet a new friend!"

Red Rover began to wag his tail as he sniffed at the puppy. Bruce's attention was still on his sister.

"What if somebody had seen you bringing those dogs in here? What if that person told Aunt Alice or Dad or Mom? How long do you think we could keep our hotel going if they found out about it? About two minutes, that's how long."

"Jerry Gordon did see us," Debbie said. "You should have heard Andi take care of him! She scared him to death, Bruce."

Delightedly she recited the story of Andi's conversation with Jerry. When she had finished, Tim was grinning broadly, and even Bruce was beginning to smile a little.

"You couldn't really have scared him," Bruce said. "It was a good try, but nobody would believe that ghost-dog story. I'm sure he didn't really turn pale."

"I don't know about that," Tim said. His eyes were sparkling with laughter. "Jerry does believe in ghosts. I found that out when some of us guys were at his place for a sleepover. We had sleeping bags on the floor, except for Jerry, of course, who had a bed, and the rest of us started telling ghost stories like at a campout. Jerry went postal! He told us we'd better shut up. Then he got up and turned on the lights and the television."

"Maybe you really did scare him, then," Bruce said to his sister. "I wish I'd been there to hear it. Still, that doesn't solve the problem of all these extra mouths to feed. We don't have the money, and you know it."

"We could advertise the pups in the paper," Debbie suggested.

Bruce shook his head. "That costs money, too. Besides, you have to give an address so people can pick up the dogs. Whose address could we give? Not this one. Not Aunt Alice's."

"It's the middle of November," Andi said. "We get our allowances on December first. We can use those to buy dog food. This time I won't spend a penny on anything else."

"What about Christmas?" Bruce asked her. "Aren't you going to buy any presents for anyone?"

"I'll write everybody poems for presents," Andi said recklessly. Then she paused. For a moment she had forgotten that she was through with writing poetry. "I'll sew things," she continued determinedly. "Pincushions and neckties and stuff like that."

"You'll have to buy material," Bruce reminded her. He sighed. "Face it, guys, it just won't work.

We're getting in deeper and deeper. The leaves are finished falling now, and there isn't any snow to shovel yet, and Tim and I are about through earning money. What are we going to do?"

A soft voice spoke. "What about charging room rent?"

Everyone turned to stare at Tiffany. They had almost forgotten she was there.

"Room rent!" Bruce said. "How can the dogs pay rent? The whole reason they're here is that they don't have owners."

"But lots of dogs do," Tiffany said. Her voice seemed to gather assurance as the idea took hold of her. "People go out of town and don't have any-where to leave their pets. I know when we went on a cruise last summer, we had to leave Ginger in a kennel. They charged thirty dollars a day."

"Thirty dollars a day!" Tim let out a low whistle. "That's over two hundred dollars a week. If we charged half that, it still would be a huge amount of money!"

"Think how many cases of dog food that would pay for!" Andi's eyes were shining. "Oh, Tiffany, that's a great idea!"

"And I know just who to get for the first guest," Debbie said excitedly. "Delaney Belanger's dog, Preston. The Belangers are going out of town for Thanksgiving. They'll have to leave Preston somewhere. Why not with us?"

"You'll have to make it sound as though it's just with *you*," Andi said. "They can't know that Preston is going to be staying at a hotel."

"Of course not. But I know the Belangers," Debbie said confidently. "I've been to Delaney's house lots of times. I know they'd rather leave Preston with me than at a kennel where he'd have to stay in a cage and wouldn't have anybody to play with him."

Tiffany was standing quietly with her hands clasped in front of her, but there was an expression of pride on her face.

Bruce smiled at her and then at his sister. For the first time in weeks the worry lines had smoothed out of his forehead, and he looked like the brother Andi had always known.

"You know, this just might work," he said. "Our new partner, Tiffany, might have come up with a plan that will keep us from going out of business."

CHAPTER TWELVE

Delaney Belanger's dog, Preston, was a beagle.

Debbie brought him over on Wednesday, the day before Thanksgiving. School had let out at noon as a prelude to the holiday, and the rest of the hotel staff was waiting to greet their first paying guest.

Preston was a lively dog and terribly strong for his size. He raced up the ramp so fast that Debbie, who was holding his leash, nearly fell on her face.

"He's a hunting beagle," she explained, handing the leash to Bruce with obvious relief. "I guess there are two kinds of beagles, the hunters and the stay-at-homes. Delaney's father is training Preston to hunt rabbits. That must be why his legs are so strong."

Preston was so excited at the sight and smell of so many other dogs that he tore around in circles. He ran from one room to another, giving shrill yelps, and bounded up the stairs and came tearing down like a wild thing.

"He sure is a lively one," Tim commented. He looked a little worried. "I hope he doesn't upset the others."

"The other dogs are used to each other," Andi said. "Friday and Red have been friends for a long time now, and MacTavish is so fat and easygoing that he likes everybody. The pups are too young to get upset about anything except not eating on time."

"Still," Tim said, frowning, "I don't much like the idea of leaving Preston free to roam around the hotel. Let's put him in his room until he calms down a little."

They had decided to let Preston have MacTavish's room on the second floor and to move MacTavish in with Friday, who was lonely now that Tom, Dick, and Hairy had gone. Tim had objected at first (he always tended to favor MacTavish), but since Preston was a paying guest, Andi insisted that it was only right that he have his own accommodations.

It took some time to get Preston settled into his room, as the smell of MacTavish was still very much in it. Preston evidently had not had much experience with other dogs, and he rushed about sniffing everything excitedly.

"Perhaps he's looking for rabbits to chase," Tiffany suggested.

It was past one o'clock by the time Preston finally settled down on his bed for a nap, and Bruce felt that they could go off and leave him. As they walked toward home, they noticed that the drapes were open behind the windows of the yellow house next to Aunt Alice's and a car was parked in the driveway.

"I guess that means we won't be able to cut through their yard anymore," Andi said regretfully. "I wonder where they've been for so long."

"Aunt Alice was saying something to Mom about how they're retired people who travel a lot." Bruce looked worried. "I wish they'd kept on traveling a while longer. They might start wondering why we're going back and forth all the time, and if the dogs start barking — "

"They don't bark much," Andi said. "They're really very well behaved." The hotel was earning money, and the problem of supporting the dogs was solved at last. She didn't intend to ruin things by starting right in worrying about something new.

Lunch was on the table when they got home to Aunt Alice's.

"We expected you before this," their mother said. "I was under the impression that school let out at noon today."

Aunt Alice's nose began to twitch as she fought off a sneeze.

"Goodness," she said, "if I didn't know better, I would say there was dog hair in this room. I think I'm going to — going to — going to — *atchooooo!*"

"Bless you," Andi said, and hurriedly brushed at the hairs on her sweater. The other dogs at the hotel were kept carefully brushed, but Preston had been shedding.

They had just sat down to their sandwiches when the phone rang. Mrs. Walker answered. When she came back to the table, she was smiling.

"That was Dad calling from work," she said. "Guess what? His training program will be over at the beginning of December, and he's been assigned to his new office."

"You mean you'll be moving that soon?" Aunt Alice's round face grew sober. "I've been looking forward so much to having you here for Christmas. Life gets lonely for an old lady when the holidays come around. There have been many times lately when I've wished that Peter and I had had children. Of course, at the time we were so involved in our work —"

Bruce and Andi, who had their mouths open to cheer, let them drop closed in astonishment. For months now all they had thought about was how wonderful it would be to move out of this crowded house where all the rules were so different from the ones they were used to. It hadn't occurred to either of them that their presence might mean something special to Aunt Alice.

And Aunt Alice's reference to her "work" came as a surprise to both of them. Had she actually held a job when she was younger? It was hard to imagine this fluttery, unimpressive little woman as anything other than a housewife. Had she been a secretary, maybe, or a bookkeeper, or a saleslady? She did have a sewing room, so maybe she'd done alterations. But she'd said "*our* work," as if she and her husband had worked together. Surely their father's uncle Peter hadn't been a dressmaker?

Mrs. Walker's face grew gentle. "Why, Aunt Alice," she said, "I'm glad you feel that way. We wouldn't want to have Christmas without you, either, and we won't have to. We won't be moving very far. John's new office is going to be right here in Elmwood! That means I may end up teaching at Andi's school."

It was then that they heard the sound. It started low and rose slowly, note by note, into a long, wretched wail.

The smile faded from Mrs. Walker's face. "What on earth is that?"

"It's a siren!" Aunt Alice's plump face grew pale. "Another air-raid warning just like the one we heard last month. Oh, dear, oh, dear, this time it must really mean war!"

"It isn't the same, though." Mrs. Walker was listening intently. "That sound we heard in the night was like an alarm going off. This is more of a — a sort of — howl. It sounds almost like a hound on the trail of a rabbit."

Bruce and Andi exchanged helpless glances as the deep, mournful voice of the beagle rose again, longer and louder this time.

"It *is* a hound!" their mother exclaimed. "I'd know that sound anywhere. My father used to have one when I was a little girl. That's the way they howl when they're hunting or when they're cooped up somewhere and want to get out."

"But nobody in this neighborhood owns a hound," Aunt Alice said. "At least, I've never heard of one. Do you children know of anyone who has a hunting dog?"

"No," Andi said weakly.

Bruce thought desperately. "Maybe it's in a car parked someplace," he said. "I could go look."

He was out of his seat and halfway across the room before his mother could stop him.

"Don't be silly!" she exclaimed. "Come back here and finish your lunch. If someone has left a dog in a car, it's none of our business. If that noise keeps up long enough the police will investigate."

"The police!" Bruce exclaimed in horror.

"Disturbing the peace," Aunt Alice said. "They have fines for that."

"I'm through eating." Andi laid her napkin on the table beside her plate. Without ever having met the elderly couple in the yellow house, she could picture them clearly, standing by their telephone, looking up the number of the police station. If Preston's howls were this loud here at Aunt Alice's, what must they be like one house closer!

"Please," she said, "may I be excused?"

The beagle's voice rose, wavered, fell, and rose, wavered, and fell again. Then, suddenly, the sound stopped.

"Well," Mrs. Walker said, "someone must have investigated and let the poor thing out."

"Please," Andi repeated frantically, "may I be excused? Please, Mom, Aunt Alice — I'm really finished."

"I am, too," Bruce said. "I couldn't eat another bite."

"Oh, all right," their mother said with a little laugh. "After all, it's Thanksgiving vacation. Run along and play, and tomorrow you can stuff yourselves on turkey and —"

They did not stay to hear the end of the sentence. Her first words had hardly been uttered before both children were out of the house and running wildly down the street toward the hotel.

They had almost reached the ramp when they saw the figure of the boy standing near it. He had his head cocked to one side and was listening intently. Bruce stopped short, and Andi, who was right behind him, nearly ran into him.

"Not him again!" she breathed. "Not here! Not now!"

Jerry Gordon turned to face them. "What are you doing here?" he asked.

"We're — we're —" Bruce began haltingly. Then he stopped himself. Why should he make excuses? This wasn't Jerry's property, either. "We've got as much right to be here as you do," he said.

"I heard a dog howling," Jerry said. "It sounded like Red. Somebody in this neighborhood's stolen my dog, and I'm going to find out who it is."

"Well, you certainly can't think we took him," Andi said. "Where would we keep him? You know Aunt Alice is allergic to animals."

"I do know that," Jerry said. "If it wasn't for that, I *would* think it was you. Things have been going funny ever since you two moved into this neighborhood."

"What do you mean by 'funny'?" Bruce asked uncomfortably.

From where he stood he could see the ramp leaning up to the window. It was half hidden by bushes, and the shadows of the trees fell across it, but it was still there, perfectly evident to anyone who knew where to look for it. Jerry's back was toward it now, but if he should turn around —

"All kinds of things are funny," Jerry said. "First Red disappears. Then Tim quits the gang. Then I see you guys walking across the street carrying lumber, the same boards Tim was going to contribute toward a clubhouse. Then your dorky sister comes by with five purebred Bulldales, and where are they now? She said she was giving them away. I can't see that anybody in the neighborhood has one. And then the rest of the gang quits —"

"The rest of the gang?" Bruce repeated.

"Don't pretend you don't know about that. After Tim quit the gang, the rest of the guys, one by one, started falling out, too. What have you and Tim been bribing them with? Neither of you has anywhere near the cool stuff I have."

"Bruce doesn't bribe people!" Andi leapt to her brother's defense. "He doesn't need to. People like Bruce just because he's *Bruce*. Did you ever think that maybe your gang just got sick of the way you treat people?"

"That dog howling —" Jerry began.

"You think it's Red Rover?" Now that she had started, Andi could no more have stopped talking than she could have turned off a waterfall. All the anger she ever had felt at Jerry Gordon came pouring out. "Well, I think so, too. It *is* Red Rover. It's his poor beaten-up ghost howling for revenge, that's what it is. If I were you, I'd run home and hide in a closet and lock all the doors and windows, because the very worst ghosts in the whole wide world are dogs."

Jerry's face grew ashen.

"That's a lie," he said shakily. "Dogs don't have ghosts. I wish you'd never come to Elmwood, you Walkers! Everything was great until you crashed in here. Why didn't you stay out West where you belonged?"

"We belong in Elmwood," Bruce said. "We like it here."

To his amazement, he realized that what he was saying was true. He turned to Andi, and he could see by her face that it was true for her, too.

"Bruce is right," she said. "We have friends here. It's home. Even if you're not born in a place, it starts being home as soon as you have friends."

"You're going to need every friend you've got," Jerry said. "I got rid of one kid in this neighbor-hood that I didn't like. I can get rid of two more just as easily. You wait and see." Turning on his heel, he stalked away.

Bruce and Andi stood anchored in place until he had disappeared from view. Then, with one accord, they rushed for the ramp. A moment later, they were inside the hotel, hurrying down the hall toward the stairway.

Tim was sitting on the steps with MacTavish on one side of him and Preston on the other.

"Hi," he said. "I see you finally got here."

"So, you're the reason that idiot beagle stopped howling." Bruce drew a long breath of relief. "We ran into Jerry out behind the hotel and got hung up talking to him. I was scared that dog would let out another blast right then."

"And the people in the yellow house are back," Andi added. "I was afraid *they* might have come over here and found Preston."

"You mean the Smiths?" Tim grinned. "Don't worry about them. They're a nice old couple, but they're both deaf as posts. They wouldn't know if Preston was howling right in their bedroom." Then his face sobered. "Other people would know, though. I could hear him all the way over at my house. Beagles don't like being cooped up. We can't risk this happening again. One of us is going to have to stay here all the time until we get him back to his owner."

"At night, too?" Andi exclaimed. "How can we do that?"

"Bruce and I can trade off," Tim said. "One night I'll tell my parents that I'm sleeping over at Bruce's house, and the next night he can tell yours that he's spending the night with me. During the daytime you girls can take turns dog-sitting."

"I don't like to lie to my parents," Bruce said worriedly. "Still, with Jerry snooping around like this —"

"I have an idea," Andi said.

The boys turned to look at her.

"What kind of idea?" Bruce asked warily.

"An idea that will keep him from bothering us forever. An idea that will keep him from ever hurting any helpless animal again." Andi's face was aglow with delight. "It's the best idea I've ever had in my life! Bruce, that picture you took of Red the day we arrived in Elmwood — did you get it made into a slide?"

"Sure," Bruce said. "I do that with all my best digitals. I like to look at them blown up big with a projector. What does that have to do with anything?"

"It has everything to do with it," Andi said. "Tim said the Smiths wouldn't know it if a dog howled right in their bedroom. But Jerry would know it. There's nothing deaf about Jerry."

Her voice was squeaking with excitement.

"The ghost of Red Rover is going to get his revenge!"

CHAPTER THIRTEEN

They planned it for midnight.

"After all," Andi said, "midnight is the spookiest time. Besides, everyone will be asleep by then — Mom and Dad and Aunt Alice and all the Gordons."

"Are you sure you can get the projector?" Tim asked.

"No problem," Bruce told him. "Dad lets me use it whenever I want it. All I have to do is ask him to let me show some slides after dinner and then not return it until morning. What about an extension cord?"

"I can get that," Tim said. "My parents have a lot of them."

They grinned at one another excitedly, hardly able to believe the thing they were going to do. It was truly, as Andi had said, the best idea she had ever come up with.

"We'll have to get Debbie," she said now. "She should be in on it, too. Why don't I invite her to spend the night? I know Mom will let me. Aunt Alice says she likes having children around."

"I'll tell my mom and dad I'm spending the night with Bruce," Tim said. "Then I'll go over to the hotel and dog-sit Preston. At a quarter to twelve, I'll meet you in front of your house." His blue eyes were sparkling. "Do you think it really will work?"

"Of course it will work," Andi said decidedly. "It has to!"

That evening was the longest that Bruce and Andi ever had sat through. Even the fact that Debbie was with them, having been given permission to eat dinner there and spend the night, did not make the hours move faster. After the dishes were cleared away, Bruce suggested showing slides, and Mr. Walker happily agreed. They spent an hour looking at pictures of the Southwest — of the big adobe house where they had lived, of the mountains stretching their purple tips into the sky, of aspen trees and tumbleweeds and arroyos. The last slide that Bruce showed was of a little brown dachshund with a pointed face.

"That's Bebe," Andi said softly to Debbie. Suddenly all the old homesickness for her pet flooded through her, as sharp and painful as it had been on the day she had said good-bye. "Oh, I wish she were here now — I miss her so much!"

"You'll be seeing her soon, honey," Mrs. Walker said, smiling. "Now that we know we're in Elmwood to stay, we'll find a place of our own and get settled and send for Bebe to be flown out on the very next plane."

"Are those all the slides you have, son?" Mr. Walker asked as Bruce turned off the projector and reached for the light. "Haven't you taken any pictures since we got to Elmwood?"

"Well, yes," Bruce said. "But I thought we could look at those another time. It's bedtime now, isn't it?"

"Already?" His mother looked surprised. "Since Andi has a houseguest and tomorrow's a holiday, I thought you might want to stay up a little later than usual and pop some corn and play games the way we used to do back in Albuquerque."

"That's okay, Mom," Andi said hastily. "Debbie and I are tired, too. I think we should all go to bed now."

"That's a good idea," Debbie agreed, giving a great yawn. "I'm awfully sleepy. I'm used to going to bed early."

"All right," Mrs. Walker said, looking more surprised than ever. "I know Bruce has been tired lately, but you girls, too? They must be working you terribly hard at school. I wonder if I should talk to your teachers."

She was still worrying out loud to Mr. Walker when the three children left the room.

Any other night Bruce would have slept the moment his head touched the pillow. Tonight, though, things were different. He could hear the alarm clock ticking through the pillow right into his ear as it always did, but he was too keyed up to let it tick him into slumber. Instead, he lay there listening, wide awake and alert to everything around him.

He could hear his parents and Aunt Alice talking in the living room. *How long*, he wondered, *were they going to stay up?* He could hear the trees rustling outside his window. He could even hear his own heart beating strongly against his chest.

It seemed forever before he heard the adults' footsteps on the stairs and their voices pitched low as they bade each other good night.

How long would it take for them to go to sleep? Huddled under a blanket, he counted the seconds, making them into minutes, sixty seconds to one minute, sixty minutes to one hour. Flicking on the light on the end table, he pulled the clock out from under his pillow and looked at the dial. Only a quarter to eleven. One whole hour to go.

He was sure that Andi and Debbie were lying awake in Andi's fold-down bed in the sewing room, whispering together, too excited to sleep, just as he was. He wished they were here with him so they could at least share the waiting.

"It will never get there," he told himself, looking at the minute hand that seemed solidly stuck in place against the face of the clock. "I'll lie here the rest of my life, and it never, ever will move."

But, as it turned out, at some time between then and a quarter to twelve, he fell asleep, and it took the muffled jangle of the alarm to bring him to.

He had been sleeping so hard that for a moment he thought it was five o'clock and time for Red's dawn run. Then, almost immediately, he remembered. Getting quickly up from the sofa, he pulled on the clothes that he had laid out on the chair beside him.

The light was on in the front hallway, and the girls were already there, waiting for him.

"We never even took our clothes off," Andi told him. "We just pulled the blankets up over them. We've been counting the minutes on Debbie's watch."

Bruce shushed her with a finger against his lips, and they put on their jackets in silence.

Debbie whispered, "The projector?"

It was standing by the front door where Bruce had left it. He drew a quick breath of relief that his father had not noticed it there and put it away.

Picking it up with one hand, he opened the door with the other, and the three slipped out into the night.

The moment the door was shut behind them, the darkness closed in from all sides.

Debbie gave a little gasp. "It's so black! We'll never find our way."

There was a sudden burst of light, and Tim spoke. "I brought a flashlight. Are you all set?" His voice was gruff with suppressed excitement.

"Did you bring the extension cord?" Bruce asked him.

"Sure did. Where can we plug it in?"

"The Gordons have an outdoor outlet on the side of the house," Bruce said. "I've seen Mr. Gordon plug in his electric grill there. Shine the light ahead of us and follow me."

Moving quietly, they crossed the lawn and stepped into the Gordons' side yard. The outlet was exactly where Bruce had thought it was. Tim plugged in the extension cord and attached the projector to the receiving end.

"I hope it's long enough," Debbie whispered.

"So do I," Tim said. "I didn't realize the outlet would be quite so far from Jerry's window. We'll just have to see."

With Bruce carrying the projector, they continued along the wall of the house. The ground-level window of Jerry's room loomed ahead of him. When they reached it, they stopped.

"Are you sure this is his bedroom?" Andi asked doubtfully. "Does he really sleep in the basement?"

"If you could see the room, you'd forget it was part of a basement," Tim told her. "It's like a private rec room with a king-size bed in it."

Dropping to his knees, he pressed his face close to

the window. "It's pitch black in there. He's sure to be sleeping. Are you ready with the projector?"

"Ready," Bruce said.

Crouching beside Tim, he set the machine in place and felt in his pocket for the slide. For a moment he was afraid that he had not brought it with him. Then his fingers closed around it, and with a sigh of relief he inserted it into the carousel.

"Okay," he said tensely. "We're ready. Let's hear it, Andi — the ghost of Red Rover! Loud enough to reach Jerry but not his parents."

Andi drew a deep breath. Then she opened her mouth and let out a howl. She started low, just as Preston had, and let the long, mournful wail rise in her throat, higher and higher. The result was so weird and chilling that Bruce felt shivers go up his spine even though he knew it was only his sister.

"Lean closer," he whispered. "The window is open about halfway. Let him have it full blast. He's got to be an awfully heavy sleeper to sleep through that."

Crowding in between the two boys, Andi howled again, her mouth close to the opening in the window.

From inside the room came a muffled, sleepy voice.

"What the heck — that crazy noise again —"

"He's awake!" Debbie whispered excitedly. "Now, Bruce! Now!"

Bruce pressed the button to turn on the projector. The beam of light shot through the window above Jerry's bed and fell upon the wall directly across from them. At first it was just a blur of light and color. In the reflected glow, they could see Jerry directly beneath the window, sitting up in bed.

"What's happening?" he demanded, the sleep gone from his voice. "What's that? Who — where — ?"

"Howl!" Bruce whispered, and Andi howled. It was the best howl so far. It rose and rose in a frightful wail and ended with a wild, tearing sound, like an animal in agonizing pain.

At the same instant, Bruce brought the projector into focus. The blur of light steadied, and into the middle of it, sharp and clear, came the face of Red Rover.

Bruce had snapped the picture with the dog looking straight into the camera lens. His proud head was lifted into the sunlight; his mouth was open slightly, showing straight white teeth. To Jerry it must have seemed as if Red's huge brown eyes were staring directly into his very soul.

For a long moment there was no sound from the room in the basement. Then suddenly there was a great shriek. It was so loud and terrified that the four listeners, crouched on the ground outside the window, nearly jumped out of their skins.

"Mom!" Jerry yelled. "Dad! Help! Help! Come here quick!"

The windows of the front room on the second floor went bright with lights.

"Hurry, Bruce," Tim whispered frantically. "His parents are up!"

Bruce flicked off the light of the projector.

"Run!" he whispered. "Run!"

No one had to be told twice. The girls were already at the boundary line that separated the Gordons' house from Aunt Alice's. Tim was close behind them. Jerry's voice filled the darkness in frantic shouts for his parents.

Scrambling to his feet, Bruce started after the others. He had almost caught up with them when he felt the projector jerked from his hands. To his horror, he heard it go crashing to the ground.

"Oh, no!" With a gasp of dismay, he knelt down and began groping about in the darkness. His hands closed upon the machine. He lifted it, and it rattled in his hands. A dark shape appeared beside him. Tim had come back to help.

"What happened?" he asked.

"I forgot to unplug it," Bruce told him. "It was stupid, but when Jerry started yelling, I just ran. When I came to the end of the cord, the projector snapped out of my grip. I've smashed it."

"Well, there's no sense worrying now," Tim said. "If it's broken, it's broken. Come on, let's get a move on! They'll be out here any minute to investigate."

The Gordons' house was ablaze with lights, upstairs and down. Every room seemed to have lights in it. Jerry's voice could still be heard shouting something about "Red's ghost! He's come back to get me!" Other voices, the soft mother tones, the lower father ones, floated across the lawn from the bedroom window.

Bruce got to his feet, clutching the projector.

"This is Dad's," he said. "And the cord —" He felt for the place where the electric cord fitted through the metal casing.

"Come on," Tim urged him. "We've got to run, Bruce!"

He whirled and broke away into the darkness with Bruce on his heels. Just as they rounded the corner of Aunt Alice's house, the door of the Gordons' house swung open.

Mr. Gordon stepped out and flicked a switch that turned on floodlights, illuminating the whole backyard.

"Now we'll see what this monkey business is all about," he said loudly. His voice carried clearly across the night to the four children who stood, panting in the shadows of Aunt Alice's rose-bushes.

"We made it," Andi gasped. "He didn't see us." There was a note of triumph in her voice.

"No, he didn't see us," Bruce said quietly, "but there's something else that he *will* see. The cord's been ripped out of the projector, and it's still attached to the extension cord, and that's in the out-let in the wall of the Gordons' house."

CHAPTER FOURTEEN

Thanksgiving Day passed quietly. It was a strange, still sort of day with the sky clear and blue and the cold of almost-winter settled over everything.

Debbie left for home soon after breakfast in order to share the holiday with her own family. The Walkers and Aunt Alice went to church and came home for the traditional turkey dinner. Then Mr. Walker brought in some wood, and they sat together in front of the fireplace to enjoy the first fire of the season. There was no sound from the hotel.

"Preston must have settled down at last," Andi whispered to Bruce in one of the few private moments they had together. "He looked really at home there when I sneaked over this morning to take the dogs their breakfast."

"Everything's too quiet," Bruce said uneasily.

"It's like the stillness before a thunderstorm. It's a getting-ready sort of feeling."

His stomach felt sick and queasy under its load of turkey and dressing.

"The projector cord is gone out of the outlet. I looked over there after church. It won't be long now before Jerry brings his father over here, and they'll talk to Dad, and the whole story will be out."

"I don't think so," Andi said confidently. "Just having the cord won't tell them where it came from. They'll guess how the ghost trick worked, but they won't know who did it. If they do come over, all we'll have to do is act like we don't know what they're talking about."

"The projector's smashed," Bruce reminded her grimly. "Do you think Dad's not going to notice that? Especially when the cord's torn out of it and a matching cord has turned up in the Gordons' wall?"

"Stop worrying, Bruce. It's Thanksgiving. We have lots of things to be thankful for." Andi would not be depressed. "The scheme worked perfectly. Just hearing Jerry scream — wasn't that worth anything? *Help! A ghost! A ghost!*" She giggled at the memory. "And Dad's going to be working right

157

here in Elmwood. Think how cool that is. We'll be close enough to keep up the hotel. Imagine if we'd had to move again halfway across the country. What would we have done with the dogs?"

"I guess you're right," Bruce said, and he tried to feel thankful. But the cold, waiting feeling remained inside him. All the rest of the day he fought it, but by nightfall it was still there as solid as ever. Something — and not a good something — was going to happen.

When the "something" did occur, it was the next morning. Andi knew about it first. The doorbell rang just as she was carrying her cereal bowl to the kitchen.

"It's probably the man from the real-estate agency," said Mrs. Walker, drying her hands on a dish towel. "When I talked with him on Wednesday, he said he'd be over first thing this morning, but I didn't know it would be quite this early."

"You mean we're going to look at houses?" Andi asked her.

"We certainly are," her mother said happily. "Aunt Alice is a wonderful, kind, good, generous person, but, oh, Andi, you can't imagine how happy I'll be to have a house of our own again!"

The man from the agency was named Mr. Crabtree. He was short and bald with a black mustache and a precise, decided manner.

"Let's see if I have your requirements correct," he said in a businesslike voice as he drew a sheet of paper from his briefcase. "You want a living room and a family room with a fireplace. At least three bedrooms. A big backyard with trees and plantings."

"That's right," Mrs. Walker said. "And if possible we'd like it in this neighborhood. I'd hate to make the children change schools again."

Mr. Crabtree frowned. "Well, that makes things a bit more difficult. Most of the houses I had listed for you to look at are in other school districts. There's one, though, the Brower place, which might be just what you're looking for. Would you like to see it now?"

"Yes, indeed," Mrs. Walker said eagerly. "I'll get my coat. Can we take your car? My husband has ours at work."

"We won't need to drive," Mr. Crabtree said. "It's right down the street."

"It's *what*?" Andi felt a sudden chill sweep over her. "Oh, Mom, no — we don't want that house! It's old. It's shabby. The yard's all overgrown."

"Houses can be painted," Mrs. Walker said comfortably, "and grass can be cut, and I like old houses. They have a nice, lived-in feeling to them. Besides, how convenient it would be to live close to Aunt Alice! We could visit her every day, and she'd never feel lonely again."

"Mom, no. Please. Let's not go over there!" Andi was almost weeping.

Her mother regarded her with bewilderment. "Of course, I'm going over there. Why shouldn't I? Really, Andi, this isn't at all like you. Don't you want to come with me? You've never seen the inside of that house, either."

"I don't — you can't!" Andi whirled and went tearing down the hall. "Bruce! Bruce! Where are you? Bruce, the thing you were scared of — it's happened!"

Bruce was in the den, trying to study. He glanced up when his sister came rushing in. One look at her face was enough to drain the color from his own.

"What is it? What's happened?" He was out of his chair in a minute. "Who was that at the door? Mr. Gordon and Jerry?"

"No, worse. Much worse." Andi could hardly get the words out. "A real-estate agent's here, and he's taking Mom to look at houses, and the first house they're going to look at is our house! The dogs' house! The *hotel*!"

"Oh, no!" Bruce was down the hall and out the door like a bullet.

By the time he had reached the sidewalk, he knew it was too late. His mother and Mr. Crabtree were already standing on the front steps of the hotel, and Aunt Alice was with them. Mr. Crabtree was fitting a key into the lock.

"It's a roomy house," he was saying. "Just the number of rooms you are looking for. The people who owned it had to leave suddenly. I think their son had some sort of emotional problem and couldn't adjust here."

"Mom!" Bruce shouted, and his mother turned to wave at him.

"Come with us, dear," she called cheerily. "We may be getting our first look at our new home!"

"It's too late, Bruce." Andi echoed his own thoughts as she caught up with him. "It's too late to do anything now except pray."

Shoulder to shoulder, like prisoners going to face a firing squad, they followed their mother and Mr. Crabtree into the familiar brown house.

The moment they were in the hallway, Aunt Alice started sneezing.

"How odd!" she said. "If I didn't know better, I'd think there was animal hair around here someplace. I feel just the way I do when — when — when — *atchooooo*!"

"Bless you," said Mrs. Walker. "Perhaps it's dust. Although it does look clean, doesn't it, for having sat empty for so many months?"

"This is the living room," Mr. Crabtree was saying. "Hardwood floors, you'll notice. The master bedroom is on the first floor also. If you'll just follow me —" With quick, efficient steps, he led the way down the hall toward the pink bedroom.

"I can't watch," Andi breathed. "Oh, Bruce, I just can't!"

She shut her eyes tightly.

A shriek split the air. "There's something in there!" Aunt Alice screamed. "It's — it's — *atchoooo*! It's a dog!"

"It's two dogs!" Mrs. Walker cried, as Friday and

MacTavish shot past her and came racing down the hall to Bruce and Andi.

"How incredible! How could they have gotten in here?" Mr. Crabtree blinked his eyes in amazement. "It seems impossible —"

From the floor above them, a deep, melodious voice broke into a howl. It rose higher and higher in a mournful beagle wail.

"That's the sound we heard the other day!" Mrs. Walker exclaimed. "It's coming from upstairs!" She started briskly down the hall.

"Wait, wait, Mrs. Walker! Don't go up there alone." Mr. Crabtree came hurrying after her. "Let me go first. It might be something dangerous." Pressing his way past her, he started up the stairway.

Andi choked back a sob. "They're going to find Preston!"

"And Tiffany's pups." Bruce's face was strained and white. "But they haven't found Red yet. I'm going back to the family room and see if I can get him out through the window. I'll hide him somewhere, even if I have to run away with him. They can't find him and give him back to Jerry — they just can't!"

Turning quickly, he ran down the hall toward the back of the house. At that moment, another scream broke forth from Aunt Alice. Preston, followed by the five joyful Bulldales, came tearing down the stairs to greet their company.

"Dear heaven!" Mrs. Walker gasped, clutching at the railing to keep from being knocked over as the string of dogs shot past her. "Why, it's — it's like a — a zoo!"

"Believe me, Mrs. Walker, Mrs. Scudder —" Mr. Crabtree appeared at the top of the stairs. His mustache was twitching nervously. "Believe me, ladies, I had no idea. I still have no idea. This has never happened before. Never at any house on our list."

"*Atchoooo! Atchoooo! Atchoooo!*" Aunt Alice leaned weakly against the wall, helpless with sneezing. Her eyes were watering so hard that great tears rolled down her round cheeks.

"You poor dear!" Mrs. Walker rushed over to put an arm around the elderly lady. "Here, let me help you! Andi, come take her other arm! We have to get her outside!"

"Here, Aunt Alice! Lean on me!" A little frightened by the violence of her aunt's attack, Andi helped to steer the wheezing woman down the hall to the front door.

She really is allergic, she thought. *She wasn't just making it up. No wonder she didn't want Bebe to stay with us.*

They stepped through the doorway into the fresh chill air, and Aunt Alice drew a shaky breath and wiped at her teary eyes.

"That was dreadful!" she gasped. "Just dreadful! All those animals! How did they get in there?"

"I don't know, dear," Mrs. Walker said. "Mr. Crabtree will find out."

"Indeed I will," Mr. Crabtree told them. Not only his mustache, but his whole face, was twitching with outrage. He pulled his cell phone out of his coat pocket. "I'll call the pound. They'll send a wagon for those beasts."

"You can't do that!" Andi burst out wretchedly. "You can't let them be dragged off and put to sleep! They're nice dogs. They couldn't help being where they were and having Aunt Alice allergic to them."

"Of course they couldn't help it," Mrs. Walker said. "Nobody's blaming the poor animals. They have no homes and nobody to take care of them.

I'm sure they were eager for any shelter they could find."

"But they do have a home! They are taken care of!" Andi cried. "Delaney Belanger owns Preston, and I own Friday, and Tim sort of owns MacTavish, now that he's gotten used to him. Tiffany owns the Bulldales, and Bruce —" She stopped herself before she got to Bruce. "They're our dogs, all of them! They can't be lugged off to the pound!"

"You and Bruce and Tim —" Mrs. Walker repeated in confusion.

"And Debbie, too. She's a partner." Andi was really crying now.

"What exactly is it that you're trying to tell me?" Her mother's voice was low and controlled. "I want the truth, not one of your stories. Are you children responsible for this menagerie? Have you been keeping eight dogs here in this house?"

"I think the count is nine," a man's voice said quietly. "Look who I found headed down the street as I was on my way home to lunch."

Blinking back her tears, Andi saw Mr. Gordon coming toward them along the sidewalk, and Bruce and Red Rover were with him.

CHAPTER FIFTEEN

It took Mr. Walker exactly ten minutes to get home from work after Mrs. Walker called him. Since his office was normally a twenty-minute drive away, it seemed to the children that the only way he could have made the trip so quickly was to have flown.

He still seemed to be flying as he leaped out of his car and strode up the walk and into Aunt Alice's house. His face was grim as he glanced about at the little group assembled in the living room.

"What in the world has been going on here?"

"You'd better ask your son and daughter that question," Mrs. Walker said as calmly as she could. "It seems they have turned the vacant house down the street into a dog hotel. There are nine dogs there now; at least, there were at last count. One of them happens to be the Gordons' long-lost Irish setter."

"A dog hotel." Mr. Walker repeated the words as though they had been spoken in a foreign language. He turned to Bruce, who was seated forlornly on the end of the sofa. "What is all this about, son? I think you'd better come up with an explanation."

"Well . . ." Bruce said slowly. How exactly had it all started? "I guess the beginning was with Friday."

"Friday is mine," Andi said. "At least, I was the one who found her. She ran in the night it was raining while you were dripping on the carpet, and she had puppies upstairs in the sewing-room closet."

"She had puppies *here*?" Aunt Alice gave a startled gasp. "There were a dog and puppies right here in this house?"

"We got them out as fast as we could," Andi said. "We didn't want to start you sneezing. And then when Bruce found out about the vacant house and that Jerry Gordon had knocked out the windows —"

"He *what*?" Mr. Gordon, who was seated in the armchair by the window, straightened up with a jerk. He was a big man and handsome like Jerry, but there was a look of kindness in his face that could not be found on Jerry's. "My son, Jerry, broke windows? Why wasn't I informed?"

"I didn't think you'd believe it," Bruce told him. "Tim Kelly said you never believe anything bad about Jerry. But the windows were out, and the house was empty, and when Red ran away and we found him —"

"And he was hurt and scared," Andi said, "and he loved Bruce —"

"— and then Andi and Debbie came home with MacTavish —"

"— and the Bulldales were going to be drowned —"

Once they were started, they could not stop themselves. The story had been building within them for so long. Now out it came, pouring like a stream rushing down a mountain. By the time they were finished, Andi was crying again and Bruce was biting his lip to keep it from quivering.

"Preston, the beagle, was our only paying guest," he ended. "Delaney Belanger's father is paying five dollars a day for us to keep him. We needed that money. The food costs have been quite high."

"I imagine they have been," Mr. Walker said

wryly. "This sounds like a pretty expensive enterprise. Nine dogs is hardly a small family."

"It's more than just food," Andi said. Now that things were out in the open, it seemed that he might as well know the worst. "We have to pay to have your projector repaired. It's smashed, and the cord's gone out of it."

"That cord was from your father's projector?" Mr. Gordon asked her. A light of understanding came into his eyes. "Things are beginning to fall into place now. You wouldn't happen to have a color slide of Red Rover anywhere around, would you?"

"Yes, sir," Bruce said miserably. "It's in my jacket pocket."

"Bruce is a wonderful photographer," Andi said. "The picture looks just like Red."

"Jerry thought so, too," Mr. Gordon said shortly.

"The thing, as I see it," broke in Mr. Crabtree, "is that this is a clear case of breaking and entering, of damage and vandalism —"

"I hardly think that," said Aunt Alice. She spoke in a businesslike manner, very unlike her usual nervous flutter. "The children did not break, they merely entered. The breaking had already been accomplished. As for damage and vandalism, I certainly didn't see signs of any. The inside of the house was clean and in excellent repair."

"That is hardly the point," Mr. Crabtree said coldly. "As I see it — "

"A house standing open with no panes in the windows is an open invitation to children," Aunt Alice continued as if she had not heard him. "It is what is legally termed 'an attractive nuisance' and is the owner's and Realtor's responsibility. The only possible charge that might stand up in court is trespassing."

She paused. Then, seeing the confusion on Mr. Crabtree's face, she continued in a gentler tone. "My husband was a private detective, and I worked with him and ran his office for many years. We had many fascinating cases and were in court a number of times. I have a good fund of legal knowledge."

Andi regarded her father's aunt with astonishment. "You never told us!"

"You never asked, dear," the white-haired woman said placidly.

"Well, *trespassing*, then. That's bad enough," Mr. Crabtree said. "What if I had taken a different buyer to see that house? How could I have explained all of those animals leaping out from all directions? I most certainly would have lost a sale, and my client might even have had heart failure."

"But that didn't happen," Mrs. Walker reminded him. "Nobody had heart failure. And you didn't lose a sale. In fact, I think you may have made one."

"The point is —" Mr. Crabtree stopped in mid-sentence. He stared at Mrs. Walker. "I beg your pardon? I don't think I quite understood you."

"I said, you may have made a sale." Mrs. Walker turned to her husband. "It's really a lovely house, dear, with nice big rooms and two baths and a fireplace. With some hard work next summer, the yard could be made quite beautiful."

"The location is good," Mr. Walker agreed. "It's close enough to my work and near Aunt Alice. I'm willing to take your word about the interior being what we're looking for. If the price is right —"

"I'm sure it will be." Mr. Crabtree looked as though a miracle were happening. "The owners are extremely anxious to sell."

"Of course, we might not be able to make a down payment if we have to pay a steep fine for our children's trespassing," Mr. Walker said. "I have to agree with my aunt that that charge is justified."

"Oh, I don't think the owners will press charges," Mr. Crabtree said quickly. "In fact, under the circumstances, I see no reason for even telling them. Since the property in question will be yours soon anyway, we can just consider that the children were 'looking it over.'"

"Which brings us to the next issue — the dogs," said Mr. Walker.

"I guess you're going to make us get rid of them," Andi said mournfully.

"I guess I certainly am." There was no sympathy in her father's voice. "Nine dogs, and then Bebe! You do still want to keep Bebe?"

"Of course I want Bebe!" cried Andi. "I love Bebe! I wouldn't give her up for anything. But I love Friday too, and they would have such good times together, and there's so much room at the hotel."

"Two dogs." Mrs. Walker spoke softly. "That's not so terribly many. I had two dogs when I was a little girl."

"Tim will take MacTavish," Bruce said. "I'm sure he will. And Andi and Debbie are training the

Bulldales for the circus. Though," he added with honesty, "they haven't learned any tricks yet. They're funny, but they're not very smart."

"We're not going to keep them until they do learn," Mr. Walker said decidedly. "Tomorrow we put an ad in the paper. Christmas is just a month away, and people always want puppies at Christmastime. You'll pay for the ad too, you kids, until every last one of those animals is gone."

The telephone rang. Aunt Alice went to answer it. When she came back she said, "Andi, it's for you."

"If it's someone with a dog," Mr. Walker said as Andi got up from her chair, "don't you dare say we'll take it."

"I won't," Andi promised.

"I'll pay for the ad, Dad," Bruce said. "I'll pay to have the projector repaired, too. I've got money put aside. I was saving it —" He swallowed hard. "I was saving it to buy Red Rover from the Gordons."

"And what made you think that dog was for sale?" his father asked him.

"I didn't. I mean, I knew he wasn't. I just —"

Bruce looked down at the floor. He could not meet his father's eyes. He did not want anyone to see that his own had tears in them.

"He wasn't for sale at that time." Mr. Gordon spoke up from his chair. "But he is now."

Bruce raised his head. "What did you say, sir?" he asked incredulously.

"Red Rover is for sale," Mr. Gordon repeated firmly. "Jerry isn't ready for the responsibility of a dog. When a boy wakes at night to a ghost, he can come out with confessions he wouldn't think of making in broad daylight. I learned a lot about my son that night — a lot that I should have known before."

He shook his head sadly. "There were people who tried to tell me Jerry had problems. I should have listened. I should have opened my eyes. It's just that when it's your boy and you love him, you don't want to admit to yourself that he's less than perfect."

"We're all less than perfect," Mrs. Walker said. "Children have to be taught the rules of living. There are a lot of those that our own two haven't yet learned."

"But they know the basic ones — kindness and sharing," Mr. Gordon said. "Jerry doesn't, and it's not entirely his fault. He's an only child, and his mother and I have tried to make up to him for that. We couldn't give him a brother or sister, so we've kept giving him *things*."

"Red isn't a *thing*," Bruce said. "He's an awesome dog. He deserves an awesome home with an awesome master."

"He does," Mr. Gordon agreed. "And I'm going to see that he gets one. Would you still like to buy Red Rover?"

"I can't afford that," Bruce said miserably. "I owe too much money already."

"I'll be willing to make up a payment plan," Mr. Gordon told him. "The important thing is to know that the dog is loved and well cared for."

"Dad? Mom?" Bruce turned to his parents beseechingly.

"Three dogs — " There was doubt in his father's voice.

"It's better than nine dogs," Mrs. Walker reminded him.

"Guess what, everybody!" A voice spoke from the doorway. It was a funny, choked-up sort of voice that seemed to be trying to keep itself steady. "Guess who you're looking at!"

There was a moment of silence. Then Mr. Walker said, "Why, we're looking at a girl named Andrea Walker."

He tried to speak lightly, but the words came out sounding strangely uncertain. The girl in the doorway was radiant, and her hands were clasped tightly before her. She looked like a person just waking from a dream.

"You're looking," she said, "at Andrea Walker, the published writer."

"Andi!" Mrs. Walker gave a cry of delight. "You've sold a poem?"

"Miss Crosno did it," Andi said in the same dazed voice. "I turned it in by mistake, but Miss Crosno liked it. She didn't tell me, but she submitted it to the school paper. They're going to publish it in the Christmas edition. It's always just the sixth graders who write for the paper. They've never used a poem by a fifth grader before, never, ever in the history of the school!"

"But they won't pay you, will they?" Bruce regarded his sister skeptically. "I thought the whole idea was that you wanted to earn money."

"Money?" Andi said blankly, as though she had never heard of the word. "There are years ahead for earning money!" Suddenly she was the old Andi again, chattering and laughing.

"This is the beginning, Bruce, just the beginning!" Her eyes were shining like stars. "I'm one week short of eleven! I'm ahead of Shakespeare!"

Read more about Andi, Bruce, and
their four-legged friends in

NEWS
FOR
DOGS

Turn the page for a sneak peek!

NEWS for DOGS

"I think we should start a newspaper for dogs," Andi said.

"You think — *what*?" Bruce Walker regarded his sister with astonishment. He had arrived home from school to find her sitting on the front steps waiting for him with her two dogs, Bebe and Friday, on either side of her. They looked like mismatched bookends, as Friday was a shaggy white hairball and Bebe, who was a dachshund, looked more like a sausage.

Elmwood Elementary let out an hour before the middle school, so Andi always beat him home, but she didn't usually wait outside to intercept him. She did that only when she had something important to tell him or when, like today, she'd come up with some outrageous project.

"I think we should start a newspaper," Andi repeated. "There's nothing for people to read to their dogs these days. Dogs need their own newspaper with articles written just for them."

"That's the dumbest thing I ever heard," Bruce said. "Even if dogs liked the stories, they couldn't buy newspapers, because they don't have money. Please, move so I can get into the house. I want to get something to eat before I take Red for his run."

Andi got up and, with a dog tucked under each arm, trailed him into the house.

"Where's Mom?" Bruce asked. Back when they lived in New Mexico, Mrs. Walker had been a teacher, but she hadn't yet found a teaching position in Elmwood, so, temporarily at least, she was a stay-home housewife.

"She and Aunt Alice went to the mall," Andi said. She set the dogs on the floor and watched with a fond expression as they raced hopefully to their food bowls. "Whatever you're going to fix, I'll have some, too. And so will Bebe and Friday."

"You can make your own sandwich," Bruce said, taking a loaf of bread from the cupboard and rummaging around for the peanut butter. "And those dogs shouldn't snack between meals. They're fat enough already." It was all he could do not to add, "and so are you," but he managed to stop himself from saying it. Andi was a little too chubby, but not exactly fat, and Bruce, although almost always truthful, was seldom unkind.

So, even though he had told her that he wouldn't make her a sandwich, he made one anyway and, then, watched with dismay as she tore off the crust and dropped a piece into each of the dog bowls. Bebe and Friday gobbled them up so quickly that they almost choked.

"See how hungry they were?" Andi said. "You may like your dog to be bony, but I want mine to be comfortable. I also want my dogs to have cultural experiences."

Bruce poured a glass of milk to wash down his sandwich and took a biscuit for Red Rover out of a tin on the dog fo od shelf. There were lots of cans on that shelf, and Bruce had bought most of them himself.

Now, as they sat at the kitchen table eating their sandwiches, Andi continued to chatter about her new grand plan.

"Of course, dogs won't buy the papers. Their owners will do that. Babies can't buy things either, but there are lots of books for babies. Parents buy them and read them to their children. That's how it will be with our newspaper."

"Don't call it *our* newspaper," Bruce said. "This is your idea. If you want to waste your time writing stories for dogs, then go for it. You're the writer in the family. You don't need me."

"But I do!" Andi exclaimed. "I need you to be my photographer and take pictures of things that dogs would be interested in."

"Like cats?" Bruce suggested, trying to conceal his amusement.

"That's one possibility," Andi said solemnly. "An occasional cat would be all right, especially if a dog was chasing it. But, in general, I think dogs would prefer to read about each another. We'll have feature stories about dogs doing feats of bravery, and a gossip column for dogs, and articles about things that dogs can do to have fun."

"And a nutrition column about how bread crusts make dogs fat?"

Bruce placed his glass in the dishwasher. He had hoped his final comment would end the conversation, but when he turned to go out through the kitchen door, Andi was right behind him. When his sister got an idea in her head she never let go.

As they stepped out into the yard, Red Rover came bounding to meet Bruce as if he had been counting the minutes until his owner got there. Or his "almost owner." Bruce was saving up to buy Red, but since Irish setters were terribly expensive, it was taking him longer than he'd expected. He had hoped that he could earn money shoveling snow, but there hadn't been any major snowstorms that past winter. Now they were well into spring, and that opportunity was gone. It seemed as if he was destined to go without an earned income until mid-summer, when people would need their lawns mowed.

"You know you need money," Andi said as if reading his mind. "We could earn a lot with a newspaper. There are so many dogs in this neighborhood, we'd have a huge readership."

"You're a nut," Bruce said. "Come on, Red, let's go!"